The
Last Ghost
Dance

Stuart L. Scott

Moscow, Idaho

The Last Ghost Dance

Stuart L. Scott

Published by
Stuart L. Scott
112 S. Main St.
Moscow, Idaho

Copyright Stuart L. Scott, 2021

ISBN Print 978-1-7322468-8-1   eBook 978-1-7322468-9-8

Printed by Kindle Direct Publishing

Cover Design by: Tania Suarez Mendoza

Front cover art illustration design copyright 2021 By Perri Duncan BA

Website : www.perriduncanstudio.com

This is a work of fiction. Many of the characters were inspired by historical research but the events are fictionalized and do not represent actions attributable to any specific person living or dead.

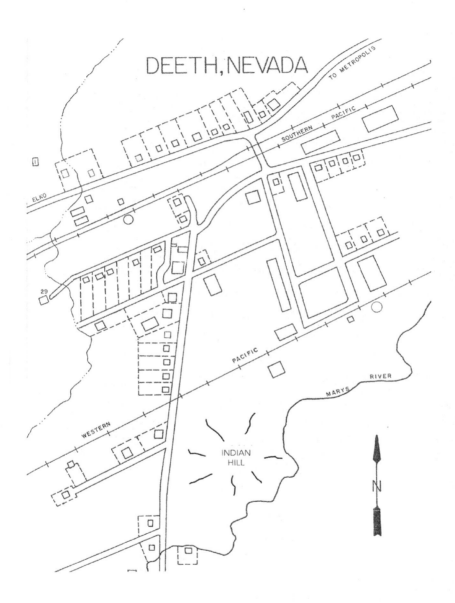

DEETH, NEVADA

Contents

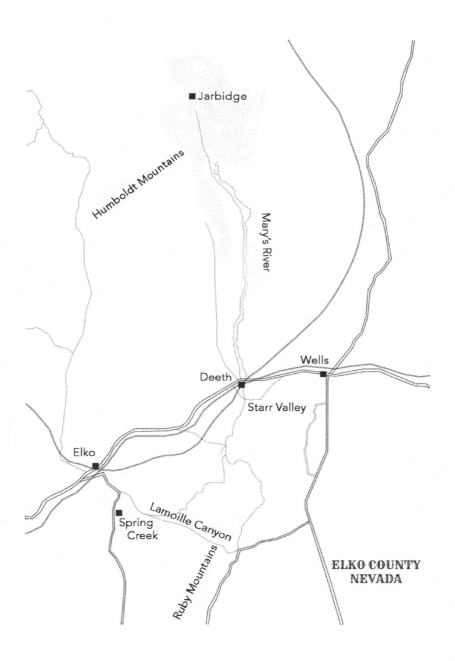

Jarbidge

Humboldt Mountains

Mary's River

Wells

Deeth

Starr Valley

Elko

Spring
Creek

Lamoille Canyon

Ruby Mountains

ELKO COUNTY
NEVADA

I dedicate this book to my four children:
Joe, Lisa, Sarah and Carey.

1.   Love and Death in a Small Town

Verrall Black sprang from the swarthy, dark *Reivers* of the Scottish lowlands, a place of constant border warfare. His beard matched the black of his hair and eyes. He stood 5 foot 9 inches tall, wire tough, the sinews of his forearms bulging beneath their canopy of black hair. His coloration lived on in his oldest daughter, Melba. His second child, Doris, had her mother's red hair and pale skin that would too soon freckle.

The Black family came to Nevada in the 1880s. Verrall Black used the proceeds from his family's success in cattle ranching to open a store in Deeth. The sign above the porch overhang read, "Deeth Mercantile—General Merchandise." The town boasted 500 souls in 1908, and his was the only store. The local Paiute band sold pine nuts and deer hide gloves to the mercantile.

Business was good, supplying the locals from Starr Valley, miners from the gold mines at Jarbidge, and cowboys from The Union Land and Cattle Company that ran over 1000 head of cattle on the sage-covered range surrounding the town.

Across the dirt street from the Mercantile was the Post Office. As the railhead for the Jarbidge mines, Deeth became the largest town in Northern Nevada. Jarbidge gold fueled an expanding local economy.

An opera house, roller rink, barbershop and ice cream parlor opened. Solidifying Deeth as a town was a two-cell city jail, a one-room school, a Chinese laundry and a boarding house and restaurant.

The boarding house was not to be confused with the "Women's Boarding House" that operated above the town's only tavern and dance hall, owned by John Hudson. Cowboys, miners and railroad men now had more opportunities to shed their burden of heavy gold coins.

Three "working ladies," Minnie, Mabel, and Lottie, rented the rooms upstairs. Hudson was their landlord, not their employer.

Lottie Loomis was a willowy brunette from California. She had left her home heading for Denver but only made it as far as Deeth. She had the looks, personality and discipline to do more than trade what she had for what she needed to get by; she aspired to operate a house of her own. She exuded seduction along with raw sexuality. Lottie's real talent was effortlessly convincing men that she wanted them as much as they wanted her. She flirted. She teased. She told every man that found his way into her arms, "You are different from all the men I've known before." Unfortunately, John Hudson believed her.

The saloon owner had set his sights on Lottie. He dreamed about her constantly, in fantasies both erotic and domestic. He took every opportunity to keep her in his sight. Lacking self-esteem, he never risked the rejection, or worse, ridicule by showing his feelings.

John had a hired bartender in the evening, allowing him to float between being a greeter and piano player. As he played his piano below, his mind couldn't escape the thought of Lottie in bed with another man just above him. One Saturday night, he watched Lottie ascend the stairs with a customer, laughing and smiling at the man. His control cracked. His eyes leaked tears as he played the ivory keys. Onward his imagination led him. She was up there now, right above his head, sharing her charms with someone who didn't love her or deserve her as he did.

His hands balled into fist and the fists crashed onto the keyboard. The clang of the keys rang out over the conversations from the barroom and dance floor. As the music stopped, so did the dancers and the talk. The room went silent when John drew out a Colt revolver from his inside coat pocket and began shooting into the dance hall ceiling. "Boom-boom-boom."

No one moved. One group of four men immediately turned their table sideways for a barricade. Ben Kuhl, a small-time thief, had just introduced his two friends, Bob McGinty and Ed Beck, to Fred Searcy, a local teamster. Kuhl believed Fred, who drove a freight wagon, might be a good man to know. He'd file away Searcy's name and his job for possible later use.

The four looked over the table top. Every eye in the room was now focused on Hudson. Adjusting his aim, he let loose again, "boom-boom-boom," emptying his gun into the pale plaster ceiling. The crowd watched as he turned away from the piano and dropped the pistol onto the floorboards at his feet. His elbows went to his knees as he wept into his hands. Drops of smelly liquid began to fall through the bullet holes and drip onto his shirt.

Ed Smiley, the bartender, finally judged it safe to approach his sobbing boss. He picked up the gun, passing it to Dennis McDermott. Ed then walked through the cloud of black powder smoke and climbed the stairs from the dance hall to the bedrooms. From the hallway, the two other doors were cracked open. Other upstairs customers, half-clad, peeked out. The door to Lottie's room was still shut. Ed paused at the door, listening. Finally, he spoke the first words since the shooting. "I'm coming in."

No one was alive inside the small room. Two naked figures lay entangled on the metal-framed bed. Lottie's body lay face down astride her male guest. Blood pooled on the bedding and the floor from two bullet wounds to her upper

3

body. Her companion was shot in the thigh. Other wound tracks, concealed by their bodies, were dripping blood onto the floor. There it mixed with the liquid contents of a chamber pot under the bed, also shot through. The ammonia from urine mixed with the iron smell of their blood.

Ed backed up, closed the door and walked down the stairs to the dance hall.

Hudson was still seated on his piano stool, head in hands. Word had spread out from the bar to the de facto leaders of the town. Verrall Black, Ben Armstrong and Bob Anderson clustered together with Dennis McDermott in the center of the room.

Ed took two steps toward the men before speaking. "Lottie and Roy Wooden, the section foreman, are both dead." Standing aside as the four men whispered among themselves, Smiley posed the unspoken question on many minds. "What's to be done now?"

Verrall Black spoke for the group. "We've been talking it over. Ben and Bob will take Hudson over to the jail for the night. We'll ask Mabel and Minnie to clean up Lottie's body and wind her tight in a sheet. You and I will do the same for Roy."

"Then what?" asked Ed.

"You get some help, maybe the other men upstairs, and move the two bodies to the cattle company shed for now. That will keep them cold and safe until somebody comes up from Elko."

Smiley nodded his agreement. The five men separated to deal with their appointed tasks. Hudson's shirt was soaked by the drops falling from above. Fate had pissed on him again.

As they separated, one of the group turned and stopped the bartender with a question. "Did she know how he felt?"

"I guess not."

4

Later Saturday night, Verrall and Ed Smiley took two blankets, a plate of biscuits and stew, hard candy and a cup of hot coffee over to John Hudson. They had no concerns about Hudson trying to escape.

"John, these should help you through the night. There's a slop bucket under the bunk. You may have already found that."

Hudson nodded that he had. He sat on the wooden bunk, staring at the cement floor, but neither spoke nor made eye contact with Black.

Verrall nudged Hudson with the plate and offered the hot cup of coffee. Hudson took both as Ed Smiley entered the cell and placed the blankets on the bunk.

As the cell door closed, Hudson looked up and gave a momentary smile. "Thank you." After a long pause, he spoke again. "They're dead, aren't they." It was not a question.

Ed Smiley delivered the answer as the cell door closed. "Yes. Both."

In the morning, John Hudson was dead by his own hand, hung with an improvised noose fashioned from strips of blankets braided together and attached to bars in the cell window. His meager last meal lay untouched on the bunk.

2.　Deeth, Nevada, 1908

"When do they stop, Momma? It's been two days already."

Sarah Elizabeth "Libby" Black looked up from her mending. Five-year-old Doris sat on the front porch. Her sister, Melba, was reading a book as she swayed the glider-swing back and forth. The six-year-old's left foot stayed flat on the porch as her leg propelled the swing: three inches forward, three inches back.

Fifty yards beyond the last row of houses, "Indian Hill" rose one hundred feet above the surrounding sage. Its flat top was now ringed by a sagebrush fence. A thin column of smoke trailed up from a fire in the center of the enclosed circle. Every year at summer solstice, the Paiute bands congregated and danced.

The Paiute shelters called wickiups filled the meadow at the base of Indian Hill. The temporary village brought 500 souls for the 'Sun Dance' for a few days before returning the site to the eight Indian families that lived there year round.

"The Paiutes call it a 'Round Dance.' They'll keep dancing for three more days, if they can. The man standing in the middle of the circle is the dance leader." Long accustomed to the annual Paiute summer solstice congregation, Libby returned to her mending.

She was lying to her daughter; a lie was necessary for five-year-old Doris. To call it by its right name, the 'Sun Dance' or 'Ghost Dance,' courted trouble for whites and Paiute alike.

In 1869 a Northern Paiute shaman, Wodziwob, had a vision of passing through the 'Land of the Dead.' In 1889, another Northern Paiute called Wovoka began preaching about his own vision. In his vision, Wovoka received the 'Ghost Dance' with instructions to bring it to his people.

The five-day Ghost Dance was the divine path to universal peace and health as it swept away all evil from the world. Hundreds of Indians danced in the giant round circle. Inside the circling dancers sat a core of drummers, beating out a rhythm. Behind the drummers sat singers, their voices tuned to the constant clock-wise circling. Two steps forward, a shuffle to the outside, then back into line.

Libby knew about the massacre of Lakota Sioux Ghost Dancers in December 1890 at Wounded Knee in South Dakota. The Ghost Dance was banned by the federal government in 1904, but it never went away; it just went underground. When Libby Belknap Black looked up from her Deeth, Nevada, porch, she saw only a harmless Paiute 'Round Dance'.

Indian Wars were within the living memory of many individuals, and all the authorities. Warriors from the Snake War of the late 1860's were still alive. In the Bannock Wars of 1878, Paiutes rebelled and lashed out at white settlers before an uneasy peace between the two communities had returned.

The prospect of tribes uniting through the Ghost Dance ceremony terrified the white government. Because the Paiutes congregated and danced at Indian Hill, Deeth, Nevada, had the potential in the minds of many whites to be a flash point. No matter what the dance was called, Ghost

Dance or Sun Dance, such mass gatherings had often been the prelude to war.

The Elko County sheriff routinely dispatched two deputies to Deeth during the dancing, just in case. Deputies Bill McCabe and Jim Graves made regular checks on the gathering. The five days of dancing, two days before and after for the comings and goings of the Paiute bands, kept the lawmen in town. Bill and Jim joked that in the event of trouble, they'd have the honor of being first to die. Verrall Black functioned as the unofficial Mayor of Deeth. Black also led a loosely organized "Citizens Civil Order Committee" that kept order in the days before the arrival of the deputies.

"The Union Cattle Company gives them a steer, one for each day, so nobody at the gathering goes hungry and gets tempted to steal to eat," Black told the deputies. "Fellas, everything is quiet. They keep to themselves, stay out of the bar and everywhere else for that matter. Hell, my store doesn't even get any business from 'em."

* * *

The Deeth Paiutes covered their wickiups in reeds gathered from the nearby Mary's River. Living side by side with the white community necessitated the adoption of some white man's practices concerning sanitation. Three wooden outhouses, each a two-holer, stood together in a row close outside the village. The Indian women found part-time work as domestics or cooks. They continued their tradition of gathering berries, pine nuts and other edibles among nature's bounty. Their husbands and single men kept to the old ways of hunting and fishing. The parallel worlds of whites and Indians coexisted as long as neither world perceived the other as a threat.

Samuel Winnemucca, great grandson of a Paiute chief, served as spokesperson for the Indians at Deeth. Six foot tall with nut-brown skin and well-muscled arms and shoulders,

8

Samuel was an imposing figure. He did repair work around Verrall's store when he was not busy hunting or fishing.

Samuel took nothing from anyone and demanded nothing. He was capable of feeding his family off the wild game from the hills and fish from the streams. He could live next to the whites without wanting to be one of them.

His wife, Pamahas, (Paiute for "Meadow") answered to Pam. She gathered the natural bounty of each season; wild carrots and onions, cattail shoots and berries, chokecherries and pine nuts. Both shared the care of the maize and squash in their small family garden. When not gathering or preserving foods, Pam used her seamstress skills to make clothing or deerskin gloves that she delivered to the mercantile.

Doris Black had renamed her five-year-old age-mate, who was Samuel and Pam's only child, 'Galli.' The little girl fit her Paiute name, Galilhai, meaning both "gentle" and "attractive." Doris and Galli played with each other's dolls. The painted porcelain faces on Doris's dolls were neither better nor worse than the stitched faces on Galli's dolls her mother had made. If their differences registered with the girls, it was of no consequence. Older Sister Melba joined in their role-playing. All three mimicked the female activities of their mothers.

Early in September 1910, Pam informed Libby that her daughters were welcome to join the Winnemucca family for their annual pine nut-gathering trip into the Ruby Mountains. Eight-year-old Melba declined the invitation, not wanting to be shackled to the two seven-year-olds. She stayed home to help her mother as an older sister too mature for childish things. Not so for Doris. If Galli went, so would she. Outfitted with a bedroll, gloves, hat, boots, and a fleece-lined canvas coat, she was off.

Before the cones dropped to the ground, men pulled them down from the trees. The pitch-covered cones were roasted over fires until they opened. Now the cones yielded their bounty of nuts, each enclosed in its own soft brown shell. Fire roasting turned the soft shells crisp. The brittle shells cracked easily, freeing the soft beige nuts. In the gathering camps, the family groups ate their fill of the soft, sweet flesh. The rest were roasted again to dry and harden them for storage.

Sometimes bands, bound together by blood or marriage, met and shared a single area or two adjoining areas. Camping together and gathering and extracting the prized nuts from the sticky cones were central rites to the larger Paiute tribe.

Around their fires at night, the families shared their news: births, deaths, and other joys and sorrows. Men shared their hunts: how deer or duck migrations might have changed. Wives shared news of whose daughter had bloomed during the past year. Who was courting whom? Had the bounty of nature been good to the family? Were the wild carrots and onions plentiful in their area? Mothers had their infants close at hand, carried on back-boards. There were cousins to visit. Younger children brought their dolls and other toys. The sharing of tradition and annual renewal of family connections made for an easy coming together of dispersed family groups.

Deeth, on the valley floor, sat at 7,200 feet. Up in the Rubies at above 8,000 feet, the weather was warm during the day but cold beyond crisp at night. Galli instructed her friend in the intricacies of eating outdoors and toileting, Indian style. While camping was known to the Black children, Paiute ways required some getting used to. Because of extensive counseling from Libby, Doris always smiled, listened more than she talked, and never set herself apart from Galli or the other children.

On the last night of the camp, good-byes were exchanged between relatives and friends, old and new, from among the bands, and they all prepared for tomorrow's trip home. Each left with multiple full baskets of pine nuts in addition to news from family and the renewal of multi-generational friendships.

Samuel, Pamela, and the girls packed the family's two horses. The adults walked and so did the girls. The path home was downhill through the pines and finally the sage. Galli and Doris walked hand in hand. The two children considered themselves sisters under the skin, uncaring about the lines drawn by either of their adult societies.

Doris was welcomed home by her mother and sister. After waving goodbye and thanking the Winnemucca family, Doris stopped outside on the porch for her mother's inspection.

"You need a bath, young lady." Libby turned to her older daughter, "Melba, go put two big kettles on the stove so Doris can have a bath." As Libby undressed her daughter from under her many layers, a sisterly voice added her opinion.

"Phew, you stink."

The young camper, now in the buff, marched inside to the bathroom. The child's skin was touched by the sun under a general patina of grime. There in the middle of her lower back a dark gray wood tick had attached itself. As mother and daughter passed through the kitchen, Libby stopped their small parade. She had the child stand facing a kitchen chair, her back to the stove. Walking back into the room, Melba noticed the tick. "Ooh!"

Doris turned, a big-eyed look of worry on her face. "What?"

Seeing Melba pointing at her back and her mother walking to the stove with a kitchen knife put Doris on the verge of panic.

"What is it Momma?"

Another "Ooh!" escaped her sister's grimacing face.

"You've got a tick on your back and we have to take it off, before it burrows in."

Doris went into full panic mode. Screaming and flailing her arms behind her back, she tried desperately to find and dislodge the monster tick.

11

"Stand still now. You don't want to knock it off. We have to get it to back out. If its head stays in your skin, I'll have to dig it out with a needle. I'll get it to back out and you'll be fine."

Libby heated the tip of the knife in the burner flame and returned to her panicked youngest. Melba watched with fascination, staring at the glowing knife and intoning a semi-swallowed "Ooh," that sounded even worse than her first "Ooh!"

"Hold still now," Doctor Mom directed as she placed one restraining hand on her daughter's back. She pressed the hot knife tip to the insect and held it against its body. Finally the tick released its bite. Libby plucked away the tick and dropped the quarter-inch-long monster to a flaming death in the stove.

Turning back to Doris, Libby finally offered comforting words. "All done, you're fine."

Hand in hand, mother and daughter left the kitchen for the promised bath. Her sobbing now ended, Doris began plotting revenge on her sister.

I'm going to pee in her shoes and blame the cat.

3. The Train Wreck, Winter 1914

The wind hurled the falling snow into a horizontal assault on the eyes and skin of any creature left to the mercies of a Nevada winter. Sheep and cattle did what they could to survive. The blinding snow stung them like so many bees, and they huddled together for mutual protection. Had anyone been there, and able to read a thermometer, it was thirty-five below zero. In days to come, calves and lambs, lacking the protection of a layer of body fat, were found frozen standing up.

* * *

Sixty-year old Dan Daniels, a retired cavalry trooper, now subsisted on scraps. He swept out the saloon and dance hall in exchange for two plates of beans and a storeroom corner for his cot. Dan cadged drinks from saloon patrons in exchange for his stories. Mixed with his bullshit was a wealth of experience that he was happy to share over a drink.

A newcomer to town wanted to know how to deal with the cold of a Nevada winter.

"The old timer will tell you, over a whisky. We call him Sarge. He was a sergeant with the 7th Cavalry at Wounded Knee," said Ed Smiley the bartender. "Hey Sarge, come over here. I've got a whisky for you."

Former Sergeant Daniels leaned his broom against the corner of the bar and stepped to the cowboy's table.

The young man extended his hand: in it the proffered drink. "Sarge, I'm told you're the man to ask. I'm up here from Louisiana and I hear it gets damn cold. Can you tell me about the cold?"

"Sure can, my young friend. It gets cold up here. Your skin freezes in five minutes at thirty below, and be sure to keep your mouth closed and covered. If you try to breathe through your mouth, your teeth will crack. You want to know what you can do for a patch of frozen skin? The answer is nothing."

"If the skin is black, it's too late. Cut it off all the way back to pink skin and red blood. What you do next depends on what you've got. Knife? Gun? Shelter? Whisky?" The old soldier stared into his whisky. "Me, I'd choose the gun."

* * *

It was January 23rd on the westbound train from Salt Lake City to Reno, when a metal brake beam snapped on the underside of a rail car. At 2:00 A.M. the sounds of the wreck were audible to Southern Pacific station agent Oliver Olson on the west side of town. The agent roused men from the railroad bunkhouse to check up the line.

"No. 5 is overdue, and I just heard a hell of a noise up north. I need you to check." Bob McGinty and Ed Beck, were silently resigned to the cold awaiting them. They headed, lanterns in hand, to an adjoining shack where the two railroad line trucks sat garaged.

14

The two headed the flatbed truck east on the dirt road that connected Elko to Wells. Just a quarter mile out of town, the lights of both the No. 5 steam engine and a chain of fires snaked out into the black night and driving snow. Bob McGinty stopped the truck. He recognized at once the enormity of the disaster and knew what needed doing.

"Ed, I'm going to the wreck. You high-tail it back to town. Tell Oliver we need doctors from Elko, every truck or wagon he can scare up, plus blankets, bandages, lanterns." The realization of what lay just ahead silenced the big man as he stared at the train-car lights blurred by the snow. "We need every man we can get. Oh Christ; get in the truck and go. I'm going up to see what I can do."

McGinty went first to the engine. The engineer and fireman were both still in the cab. Engineer Charlie Dunn was sitting on the round metal stool he usually occupied. Blood dripped down his forehead from a horizontal gash above his right eye. Likely concussed, Dunn didn't move from his stool as his head repeatedly lolled forward and then jerked back. Jack McCaffrey, the fireman, cradled his forearm but turned to face Bob as he climbed up onto the engine.

"Something broke at the number two car." He paused, his eyes opening and shutting as they refocused. "Whatever broke dang near threw us off the track."

"I've sent word back to telegraph up and down the line for doctors. We're getting help organized from town. I'm going to the wreck to do what I can until help arrives. Can you see to Charlie?" said McGinty.

McCaffrey nodded that he could.

"How bad are you hurt?"

"Busted arm from hitting the side of the cab and probably a couple of cracked ribs. I'll be fine. You see to the passengers. Get those fires out and everybody to shelter. The people in those three Pullman cars are probably in their night clothes. Go."

15

McGinty called out at each car for any porters or conductors to sing out. As he found crew members, he stepped up to making decisions and issuing orders. At that moment, there was no one else except the injured.

Cooks, porters, waiters and the bartender from the Club Car were put to work. Only half of the fourteen men on the crew were uninjured. The fires from oil lamps spilled or broken in the wreck were smothered where possible. McGinty assessed each car he passed. Emergency lanterns stowed on each car, if undamaged, were lit. As he found survivors, McGinty asked about injuries and pressed crew and passenger alike into tearing up bandages for the many cuts.

It took just forty-five minutes for the first help to arrive from Deeth. Even in the blizzard, the citizens came anyway, with wagons, lanterns, blankets, coffee and whisky. They transported everyone back to Deeth, among them four severely injured passengers. They left the body of the one dead passenger where it lay until morning. The railroad sent another train up from Carlin, Nevada. Early in the still dark morning, the passengers from No. 5 were re-boarded and moved to Carlin, where they were doctored, warmed and fed.

Bill and Ed considered themselves heroes. Nightly in the bar McGinty broadcast this perspective. Among his many listeners was Ben Kuhl. Ben was keeping a weather eye open for potential recruits for whatever plan he developed.

"Our action saved lives when the train wrecked north of town. And our thanks? A reward? A promotion? Nope, a hearty 'well done!' Nothing more."

Ben Kuhl nodded in agreement. "They don't appreciate you fellas. It's just not fair, by God."

16

Behind the Deeth Post Office was a shed and horse corral for the supply wagon that operated between Deeth and Jarbidge. Goods for the tent city that sprang up after the gold strike rode up in the same wagon as the U.S. mail in the twice-weekly overnight run.

Fred Searcy drove the contracted U. S. Mail wagon. He was as honest as the next man, if the next man had a streak of larceny. When Fred met Ben Kuhl, he became captivated by Kuhl's criminal exploits. Kuhl's self-serving tales of crime portrayed him as a mastermind, clearly smarter than all the law in Nevada. Had Searcy known the truth, Kuhl would have been unmasked as a failed petty criminal. Had Kuhl possessed any sense at all he'd have gone straight, because he was a failure at being a crook.

Searcy's job driving the mail wagon on its twice-weekly run provided him a shack between the coach shed and horse corral. Who hatched the plan to rob the Jarbidge mail is unknown. Both Searcy and Kuhn shared a belief that they were smarter than most. They also believed that their lack of financial success was not their own fault. They had been treated unfairly by the world and that was about to change.

They met in Searcy's shack, where Kuhl had lately moved in. As the two drank their whisky under the yellow lantern light, seated at the table, a plan emerged. Searcy was the perfect inside man for Ben Kuhl.

Searcy laid it out for them. "The Winfield Bank sends the North Star mine payroll, $4,000 in bills, on the train from Elko every two weeks. And Newt Crumley, who owns the Jarbidge saloon, sometimes sends up money for the Faro tables from the bank in Elko."

Searcy stared into his whisky. "The road up to Jarbidge, after it turns off the Elko-Wells road, is just a narrow track along the bank of Mary's River. The canyon is steep and there'll be twenty or thirty foot drifts along the way when the snow hits. It takes me all day to make the run, so I overnight in Jarbidge, and that's pushing my ten-horse team for all they are worth. I sure as hell don't want to spend the night outside in the wagon. Crumley's bar keeps a cot in their storeroom and I kick em' back four bits for the bed and two bits each for two meals."

Kuhl listened and planned as the two men drank. "We're going to need some more men. Think about it; you are driving and you've got your revolver and the sawed-off shot gun. Nobody is going to believe that you gave up to one lone gunman. I think we need at least two more guns. That's a story you can sell." Kuhl smiled at the genius of his own forethought and planning.

"I see what you mean. That way, I had no choice and when I make it into town, I'm just lucky that I didn't get shot."

Their glasses empty, Searcy drew their planning to a close. "I need to eat. Come on, let's go get supper at the saloon and think about who we can get to ride with us."

* * *

Bob McGinty and Ed Beck were obvious candidates. During the next three weeks Kuhl and Searcy stoked their feeling from unappreciated into aggrieved. After that, their recruitment to the plan was easy. McGinty and Beck were only to be window dressing at the robbery, and neither knew the full scope of Kuhl's plan.

Their anger and the promise of easy money enticed the two from the straight life of the rails to the crooked path of crime. "All you have to do is to be along with me when I rob the wagon," Kuhl explained. "Be visible and armed, so Fred here has no choice but to give up the mail bags without a fight."

"That's all?" questioned McGinty in a whisper as he leaned toward Kuhl across the barroom table. Beck also leaned in to hear this crucial answer.

"That's it. We ride up, camp, and wait. You two stand in front of the wagon so your guns are visible. I'll go down to the wagon and get Fred to give up the two mail satchels." Kuhl paused, looking over at Searcy and smiling at his own ingenuity.

"I don't get why you need us at all. I mean if we stop the wagon before town and Fred's in on the plan, why do you need us standing around?" McGinty pressed.

"We need more men with guns because Fred never knows until the morning when he picks up the cash, if there's going to be a passenger with him. A passenger would actually be a good thing, because he'd be a witness."

"OK, I can see that. It puts Fred in the clear when the money is stolen. But tell me this," McGinty paused to craft his thought into a clear question. "If there is a passenger who sees the whole thing, how do we get away with the money? Explain that to me."

"See, you three are lucky that I'm in charge here. Here's the genius part of the plan. Fred is going to rig a false bottom under part of the wagon bed. When we're at the back of the wagon, you make sure that any passengers ain't watching us."

"Why," asked Beck. "What does it matter?"

19

"Fred and I will dump the cash into the false bottom under the wagon bed. The passenger, our witness, sees us with our guns on Fred and is going to think we rode off with the mail bags." Kuhl paused to sip and bask in his own admiration.

"But why not just take the money with us then? Why do all this play acting about hiding the loot in the wagon?"

Kuhl was getting frustrated with McGinty's questions but concealed his growing frustration. Why couldn't they recognize his criminal expertise?

"Well, we don't know how much weight we'll be packing out and our horses might be belly deep in snow. If the bar is sending up money for the Faro table, sacks of coins can get mighty heavy. Besides, if the law finds us on our way out of the canyon, they've got nothing to connect us to the robbery."

"We'll stop the wagon a good hour from Jarbidge so we've got time to get well away. The three of us are masked. We hide the mail sacks and ride off. The next day Fred drives the wagon back to Deeth with our money hidden inside. We meet back here and you get your cuts." Kuhl turned to the other three, holding his gaze until each man nodded. The four clinked their glasses together as a sign of mutual agreement and parted ways at the saloon door. They'd meet again when Fred signaled the time was right.

* * *

What folks say about "No honor among thieves" didn't originate with Ben Kuhl. He just reinforced the wisdom of the old saying.

Fred Searcy rigged a small false bottom under the rear corner of the wagon box. As its driver and caretaker, his access was unlimited. The arrival date of the next payroll was December 5th. Besides the mine money, Newt Crumley was sending up both his payroll and cash for the gambling tables in the Success Bar. With any luck, Crumley's money would add another thousand dollars to their haul.

The robbers had four days to set their plan in motion. Kuhl and Searcy had already scouted the Jarbidge Canyon road. They agreed on a spot for intercepting the stage. One hour from town, a side canyon joined the river road where a small creek added to the larger flow. The ground flattened out opposite the snow-covered creek bank. A stand of willow trees by the creek offered concealment. The confluence of the creek at the river was a landmark for their rendezvous with the two hirelings.

Kuhl told McGinty and Beck the December 5th date. They had enough time to arrange alibis covering their absence from town. McGinty was a supervisor, so scheduling time off was easy. Beck received two days off work to "deer hunt." The four agreed to meet at the creek at noon on December 5th.

Fred Searcy's day began in the early morning as he harnessed his ten-horse team. Driving the short distance through town to the Southern Pacific train station, he signed for the mine payroll shipped up on the train from Elko. He also signed for $3,000 in bills and $300 in silver for the Crumley operations. Searcy loaded the two payrolls into the U. S. Mail sacks that were already in the wagon box and covered the box with a tarp.

A passenger for the trip also waited at the station: Clarence Cornwall, a foreman at the North Star mine.

The wagon trip was uncomfortable but the only way to get to Jarbidge other than an all-day horseback trip. The passenger and driver agreed that they'd probably run out of ass before they ran out of road.

"We'll be in Jarbidge about 5:00 P.M. in time for dinner," Searcy advised just before pulling out of town at 6:00 A.M. The morning was cold and clear. The snow extinguished the ever-present smells of sage and juniper that filled the desert air for most of the year. The road, for the first traveler of the morning, was only marked by frozen ruts showing beneath

21

the most recent snowfall. The frozen breath of the horses fanned out into a brief trailing stream as the wagon headed up the road.

Three hours into the trip, they stopped to rest the horses and give driver and passenger a chance to pee on a tree of their choice. Then they continued up the canyon along the river. As Fred Searcy held the reins of his ten-horse team, time ticked off the countdown to the robbery.

Honest as the day is long, especially just two weeks before the shortest day of the year, Searcy began to plot his own robbery plan. Could he rob his partners of the Crumley money which they didn't know about? Thirty-three hundred from Crumley, plus his share of the $4,000 would set him up good.

Was the extra money worth the risk? How long would it be before everyone knew both the North Star and Crumley payrolls were stolen? As he drove, Searcy's greed battled with his fear of Kuhl.

The snow blowing into his face blurred his vision and numbed the band of skin between his upturned fleece collar and the hat he'd pulled down to just above his eyes. Driver and passenger shared a heavy lap robe that covered their legs, keeping them warm and dry from the blowing snow.

Kuhl, McGinty and Beck waited in their hiding place among the willows. They knew within an hour when the wagon would arrive. When they heard the approaching team coming up the canyon, the three took up positions across the narrow dirt road. Showing off their number and their guns was key to selling the plan to any passengers.

Searcy drove the wagon around the last bend before the ambush site. There was Kuhl, standing in the middle of the road with his rifle shouldered and aimed up at the driver's seat. Searcy reined in the team, loudly shouting, "Woah-woah-woah," as the wagon bucked and swayed. McGinty and Beck, both armed with rifles, stood plainly visible just ahead, one on each side of the snowy road.

Clarence Cornwall spoke under his breath. "I've got my pistol inside my coat pocket. What do you want to do?"

"I've got my pistol and the shotgun but there's three of them. I say we give up what they want," Searcy directed his passenger.

McGinty and Beck stood fast, rifles at the ready. Kuhl approached the wagon, walking through the fog of steaming breath from the team, leading his horse behind him.

"Driver—climb down. Don't be a hero. We want nothing of yours." As Searcy clambered from his seat, both men played their roles for the passenger to hear and clearly see.

"We want the mail sacks."

Searcy kept a brave face as he walked in front of the armed robber back to the rear of the wagon. Kuhl looked at the passenger as he passed. With his hat pulled down and a bandana over his face, he fixed Cornwall with a momentary hard stare.

"Get on down and stand in front of the team." Then he added, "We don't steal from folks like you."

The crime partners folded back the tarp covering the wagon bed and pulled out the mail sacks holding the payrolls for the mine and the saloon. They shunted freight to one side as Searcy lifted the removable board in the wagon bed to access his hidden subfloor. Ben Kuhl drew a folding knife from his coat and used it to slit the canvas mail bags. He passed Searcy two smaller leather money bags, one from each payroll. Each held bundles of paper money. The money bags were dropped into the hidden space under the boot. Then from the other mail pouch, he removed four canvas bags, each emblazoned 'Winfield Bank' and heavy with coins intended for the saloon. The coins joined the bills in the boot's subfloor. Searcy replaced the loose board and turned to go back in character as the victim driver. Kuhl left his horse, supposedly loaded with the loot, at the back of the wagon.

As Searcy walked back to the front of the wagon, followed by the rifle-toting Kuhl, he made his choice. He would rob his partners of the Crumley money, but that meant killing Ben Kuhl, who'd seen the money. He would also kill McGinty and Beck if they interfered. When he climbed back up on the wagon he'd make his play.

Ben Kuhl, the more experienced of the thieves, was keeping a steady eye on Searcy, as his partner should have been keeping on him. Larcenous by nature, Kuhl expected the same from his crime partners. When Searcy seated himself up on the wagon and turned, his pistol in hand, Kuhl didn't hesitate to shoot. "Boom," sounded the rifle as 200 grams of lead pierced Searcy's chest.

McGinty and Beck brought up their rifles as they surveyed in wide arcs around themselves, unsure where the shot had originated. Was the law coming upon them? Was it Indian marauders intending to steal from other thieves?

Kuhl climbed up to the height of the driver's seat and placed his hand on Searcy's bloody chest, checking for any sign of life. He found none. "The son-of-a-bitch drew down on me. I had to shoot. Let's get out of here."

He took the short-barreled shotgun from its resting place below the seat and extracted the two shells from the barrels. He removed Searcy's side-arm and pitched it into the river. Face to face with Cornwall now, Kuhl asked, "Do you have a gun mister? If you do, I want it now." Clarence nodded at the killer and gestured towards his coat pocket. "All right, pull it out; two fingers only, and then toss it into the river. Understand? Stay right there now, while we get out of here and you won't get hurt."

Cornwall signaled his understanding and slowly, carefully complied.

Kuhl had jumped down before noticing his bloody hand. He walked to the back of the coach and cleaned it off on the outside of a canvas mail sack. Then the two bandits walked away. They joined Ben Kuhl, walked back to their horses, and rode off down the canyon road.

* * *

As the North Star mine foreman, Clarence Cornwall knew the canyon road well. He judged the wagon to be three miles from town. As the snowfall increased, Clarence decided to walk into Jarbidge.

The driver was clearly dead; his body now slumped forward. The road ahead had a foot of new powder that flew up behind Cornwall's steps. With his hat pulled down and coat collar turned up, he trudged on up the road. He kept his gloved hands under his arm pits, rather than in the coat pockets. The frozen snow under the new-fallen powder caused him to slip repeatedly when his foot hit the crest or slope of a hidden wheel rut.

* * *

Jarbidge Postmaster Scott Fleming was starting to worry. The mail wagon was two hours overdue. A foot of snow had fallen at Jarbidge that day. The wagon sliding off the road into the river or being buried by an avalanche were both worrisome possibilities. Fleming organized a search party.

They met Clarence Cornwall less than a quarter mile from town. He described the robbery and the killing of Searcy. Clarence agreed to walk the short remaining distance into town so the riders could head on to the wagon.

The rescue party found the wagon, with Searcy's snow-covered body still on the driver's seat. As the snow continued to fall, Frank Leonard, leader of the rescue party, decided that a search of the scene could wait till morning, so he headed the riders and the team of horses back to town.

* * *

Ben Kuhl and his gang of two made it down the road another ten miles before the raging blizzard made them seek shelter. McGinty spotted an abandoned miner's cabin built low to the ground, 100 feet up a side canyon. The three settled in for the night. With horses behind the cabin there was no food for man or beast. Inside the cabin, they found paper, kindling and a stash of firewood. With shelter and fire, they settled down to wait for first light and a break in the weather.

The next day Frank Leonard, leading an armed search party from Jarbidge, returned to the wagon with the team to move it. They found the mail pouches outside the coach under the coat of new-fallen snow. Both pouches were cut and the paper money and coins removed. One pouch had a bloody hand print on the flat of its canvas. They loaded the bags inside the wagon box for transport. The driver's body, now stiff from rigor and cold, was moved to the wagon box and the ten-horse team was hitched to the wagon and taken back to Jarbidge. Fred Searcy made his last ride on top of $7,300 in stolen money.

The riders believed that the storm which had stopped them the night before had probably stopped the robbers as well. The posse headed down the canyon road in search of Searcy's killer. They moved at a slow enough pace to keep a constant eye out for signs of a camp.

Daylight came late to the canyon's bottom. Kuhl, McGinty and Beck were still asleep when the posse surrounded the cabin. Kuhl's plan, feigning ignorance of the robbery and killing, was shredded when the blood on his coat sleeve was noticed. When he was forced to show the palms of his hands, still partially caked with Searcy's blood, his alibi was debunked.

The three were arrested and taken back to Jarbidge by the posse. With neither telephones nor telegraph available in the Jarbidge mining camp, Leonard sent a rider back to Elko. Back at Elko, the robbery and killing were big news.

Elko County Sheriff Abarran Escuraga ordered a team of deputies back to the mining camp.

The next day, the three bandits were chained together and transported back to Elko in the very wagon they'd robbed. Their loot was so near but yet so far away.

The three stood trial in Elko. McGinty turned State's Evidence and testified against his crime partners. Both McGinty and Beck professed their ignorance of any plan to kill Searcy. They thought they were mere props being used in Kuhl's plan. Beck received a ten year sentence. Bill McGinty, in exchange for his testimony against Ben Kuhl, and being judged a mere pawn, was not charged and walked out of court a free man.

* * *

Two forensic experts from California matched the bloody palm print on the mail pouch to Ben Kuhl's hand. Kuhl was sentenced to die. Kuhl refused an opportunity to save his own life by revealing the location of the stolen payroll monies. He declined, believing that the authorities were trying to trick him. "Change my death sentence to twenty years first and then ask me," was his answer. Ed Beck was also offered a small reduction in sentence if he gave up the location of the stolen money. His reply mirrored Kuhl's.

When the carrot didn't work, Newt Crumley and bank president George Gott decided to try the stick. Their political connection, the Warden of the Nevada State Prison, got his palm appropriately greased. Two hard rock miners from Carlin, Nevada were hired to pay Kuhl and Beck a visit inside the Carson City prison.

Kuhl was visited first. Miner Joe Johnson came straight to the point. "Give up the money or we beat the livin' shit out of you." Kuhl only smiled, and told the pair to do what they had to do, because he wasn't talking. And they did. And he didn't.

Then the two visited Beck. Their same question was again asked and answered. Kuhl and Beck were both left unconscious and bleeding on the floor of their cells. Each man took the beating because they counted on future larger offers of reduction in their sentences. If they gave up the location of the loot, they'd forfeited that chance.

The total of $7,300 had not been found. Reluctantly, Crumley and bank president Gott agreed to post a reward for the return of their money. It was painful, but they had to offer an amount that did not encourage any searcher to conceal the find and keep the full $7,300. They decided to offer $2,500 and published their offer in newspapers throughout the West.

* * *

The mail wagon sat back in Deeth while Kuhl and Beck were on trial in Elko. The robbery loot was still hidden aboard the wagon. The company brought in a new driver to replace Searcy.

McGinty returned to Deeth after his trial testimony and release. He'd been fired from the railroad job but he wasn't concerned. There was a fortune waiting under the floor of the wagon bed. McGinty camped outside of town and watched for an opportunity to get at the holdup loot. The wagon was back in its usual shed, next to the horse corral and behind the post office. Little did he know his simple plan was about to take a complicated turn.

5.   Hide-and-Seek, 1916

One Saturday in April, it was chilly but sunny, and after a week inside the classroom, the outside beckoned. With coats, mittens, and caps on, the kids set 'home base,' how much time they would get to hide, and the boundaries of the game area. No fair hiding on Indian Hill, or across the creek or Mary's River. They could only hide inside the boundaries of town.

Doris and Melba Black were in the game. So were the McDermott boys. Jimmy McDermott wore his right arm in a sling after falling out of a second-floor window in the Elko County Court House.   Even children's play could be dangerous. Six other kids including Galli Winnemucca were also playing the game.

Melba Black was first to cover her eyes and count while everyone else hid. "One, two, three..." and on her counting went, all the way to 100.

"Ready or not, here I come." And the game was on. Nine kids stole glances from their hiding places, waiting for Melba's search to take her far enough away from her base for them to race past her and be home safe. Melba walked soft-footed, trying to catch them unawares. Velma Truett peeked from behind a rain-barrel next to the ice cream parlor. Marita Ryan watched from her spot amid the cattails on the creek bank as Melba found her and tried to out-race her back to tag home. Melba won.

Twelve-year old Galli Winnemucca watched from her hiding place, kneeling inside the mail wagon. The wagon shed roof put her face in shadow. Three feet above the shed floor was a good vantage point for peeking over the side of the wagon box. Galli kept returning to this spot, as yet undiscovered by her playmates in any of their past games.

When her lower leg started to numb, she scooted her foot back. The three-inch move was just enough to put weight on the back of the loose board in the wagon bed. Invisible from above, the cross-bracing of the wagon frame worked as a fulcrum. The front of the board tipped up as her toes pushed the back of the board down. Galli kept her focus on the game, ignoring the loose wood on which she knelt.

As the game drew on, Melba Black passed outside the wagon shed. She peeked around the side of the shed looking for anybody who might be hiding inside. Then Melba knelt down to discover anyone hiding under the wagon, waiting to race past her to home base. But no one was there, and Melba snuck off to continue her search.

Galli now felt safe to exhale; her spot was still undiscovered. She slid over, reached down and examined the tippy board under her leg. She levered up the loose board and moved it aside. Instead of seeing the shed floor below, there was a compartment, dark with shadow. Curiosity got the better of her, and she reached down into the dark. Cold metal touched her finger tips. She carefully explored the shapes with her fingertips. When the girl withdrew her hand she clutched a bright silver dollar. She carefully examined the coin. There in her hand was real money!

* * *

The game, the girl and the discovery of his hidey-hole were all unknown to Bill McGinty. Picking Saturday, his first full day back in Deeth, to claim the loot, he slipped in from his camp northwest of town. The wagon shed and corral backed on an undeveloped block at the edge of the sage. The few buildings nearby all faced away from the corral and shed. McGinty watched silently from the rear corner of the wagon shed. At six foot tall, he could see over, but not into the wagon box.

Galli Winnemucca began pulling out handful after handful of cold silver coins. Checking that she was unobserved, she lay down on the wagon box floor. Reaching into the dark of the treasure trove she searched its back corners. In the far corner her hand touched one and then a second lump. Not metal: wood or cloth. She pulled out the first of the two Winfield Bank leather cash bags.

Galli searched the back of the hiding place. She ran her fingers flat over its bottom, so as not to miss any coins. All that remained were ripped cloth coin bags. Rolling onto her side, she unzipped the heavy metal closure on each of the leather bags. Unaware of how much money she'd discovered, Galli was thumbing the stacks of bills like playing cards. McGinty reached over the side of the wagon box and put his hand over her mouth.

Galli dropped the sheaf of bills and grabbed at the hand. McGinty had no plan. The child was an unexpected problem of the worst kind. He needed to keep her quiet. His other hand flipped open a jackknife, which he brought over the top of the side rail. He whispered to the child. "Be quiet and keep still. I don't want to hurt you. I just want my money."

Galli's eyes widened as her surprise changed to fear. She kicked the wagon side-board as she squirmed. Her hands tried futilely to dislodge the hand from her mouth. Her life depended on screaming for help or freeing herself from the big stranger's grip. McGinty pressed the point of the knife blade through her canvas overalls into her skin. The sharp pain of the knife point only made Galli squirm more, but her kicking stopped as the blade point pierced her knee.

McGinty leaned in, his eyes now growing large. "Stop fighting and don't kick. You'll get cut more if you kick again." He looked away, checking both open ends of the wagon shed, fearing discovery by a random passer-by. "Shut up now." McGinty closed his eyes, and they both went silent.

Jesus, I need to think. God damn it. I can't leave her here and I can't leave without the money. As soon as she's free, the entire town will know.

McGinty had no time to plan. He couldn't run fast or far enough to get away if he released the girl now. To get the money, he had to take the girl. When he opened his eyes, her gaze was still locked on his unmasked face. He squeezed her cheeks, commanding attention.

"I can't leave you and I can't leave my money. I won't hurt you, girl, if you keep quiet and mind me long enough to get out of town. I'll let you go as soon as I'm away from town. Please." He relaxed his grip on Galli's face. "I promise I won't hurt you if you just keep still."

The captive girl breathed in short, shallow gulps of air. Her captor was panting from the combination of adrenalin and uncertainty. Their rigid forms both began to relax and the release of tension communicated through their hands and faces.

"Please," he repeated. That one word eased the tension that kept them locked rigidly in place. "Please, I promise to let you go, if you keep still. Can you do that?"

Galli nodded her head a fraction of an inch and McGinty released his grip on her face and slowly pulled his hand back. He removed the knife point which had pierced her overalls and skin just enough to make its presence painfully known.

"Your knee has just a tiny scratch. You ain't gonna bleed more than a drop." Minutes had now passed and McGinty feared accidental exposure. Believing that the girl was cowed into compliance, he started giving her directions.

"Put the paper money back in one leather sack and pass it to me. Those dollar coins are for you when you come back after I'm gone. See?" Galli passed him the money bag. McGinty stuffed the bag inside his shirt, so his hands remained free. He quickly removed his leather belt; doubling it over once and then again, he stuffed the belt into his coat pocket.

"I keep my promises. Do you? You ain't gonna run away are yuh?"

She shook her head.

"All right then, you're coming out of the wagon now. You lean over the side-board and I'm going to lift you out."

Seeing her eyes widen with uncertainty, McGinty added, "That's all I'm gonna do; promise." When the girl leaned

32

over the board, he reached under her arms and lifted her down to the ground. Then he looped his belt through the two straps on the shoulders of her bibbed overalls. The improvised leash gave him both control and freedom of movement for their escape. He pointed out the back side of the open-ended shed.

"This way, and you'll be free real soon. You promised to be quiet now." Again Galli nodded her "yes." Crouching low, robber and child crossed the final undeveloped block of town and disappeared into the sage on the other side.

* * *

"Ollie-Ollie-in-free!" called Melba Black and waited as two of her final three playmates walked towards her. As the two reached home, Melba issued her cry one more time. Galli was not back. *Why?* wondered Melba.

Melba spoke to the eight other players. "Well, either she cheated and hid out of bounds, or she probably fell asleep. We better go find her so we can start a new game. Call out when you do and we'll meet back here."

The nine children set out in all directions, calling Galli's name as they searched. "Galli, you can come out now. We won." They asked other kids as they passed. "Have you seen Galli?" After a half-hour of looking, all nine kids met back and with regret decided it was time to call in the grown-ups.

Melba hesitated in the kitchen door. "Momma, we can't find Galli. She's still hiding and won't come out." Fixing some responsibility on the lost child seemed a good way to lessen everyone else's responsibility. Libby Black was patient in her questioning of both girls. Between the length of the game and the time of the search, Galli Winnemucca had not been seen for an hour. As her concern grew, Libby told her girls to go clean themselves up while she went over to the store and told her husband what she knew.

Verrall decided he needed to find Samuel Winnemucca and alert him that his daughter had gone missing.

"First, I want to talk to the girls. I'll close up the store and be right over." Verrall considered what might have happened to Galli. Bears and mountain lions did occasionally come down from the Ruby Mountains. Galli was on the verge of being old enough to attract the attention of some young buck from another Paiute band. The Mary's River was running high and the memory of poor Bessie Grock, who drowned in the river last year, came to his mind. There was no end of terrible possibilities, from snakes to a bad fall. The world was a dangerous place.

* * *

McGinty led his young captive through the sagebrush and juniper cover. He planned to head up Jarbidge canyon. North of town the pair had to cross a set of railroad tracks, which meant leaving the cover of the sage. He and his captive waited in the brush until McGinty thought it safe, then he led her across the tracks into the cover on the other side.

He kept her moving for an hour. When the girl stumbled, he knew she had to rest, be carried or be killed. McGinty was not proud of having become a thief, or of succumbing to how Kuhl had bragged on his life of crime. Yes, he'd been tempted and given in to the prospect of quick money for just looking dangerous. On the run now, and with a young girl in tow, he silently asked himself; *How the hell did I get myself into this God damned mess?* Knowing he could not undo this mistake didn't ease his mind. *What do I do with the girl?*

He slowed their pace to a walk and then halted. "We're going to rest here." He expected her to be crying, but her eyes were dry and her face empty of any expression. Still controlled by the loop of McGinty's belt, Galli sat down on the sandy desert soil opposite her captor. She looked back along their trail. The ever-present smell of sage came to their nostrils as they sat, hiding and resting.

McGinty heard the big diamondback before he saw it. The enormous rattlesnake lay coiled next to the sage branches a foot behind Galli. Its broad, triangle-shaped head rested low over the thick, coiled body that was already arched upward, a coiled spring ready to release. Twelve dried buttons adorned its tail, one for each year of life. McGinty knew that if Galli tried to move the snake would strike. His mind raced, searching for an answer, an escape, any type of plan.

Galli stiffened when she heard the snake buzz. Only staying frozen in place was keeping her alive, at least for the moment. Her blank expression changed and her eyes beseeched the adult for help. McGinty was slowly moving his head, casting his gaze about for a weapon. There was no big stick or rock within reach. Except for skinny dead sage branches, he had nothing but his wits to arm himself with.

The rattler buzzed its warning again as he slowly unbuttoned his canvas coat. Then McGinty unbutton two buttons on his shirt and reached inside. He had no gun, and the blade of his jackknife was useless. All he had as even a faint hope was the leather money bag he'd carried away from Deeth. As he withdrew the bag from inside his shirt, McGinty, as calm as he could manage, spoke to his captive.

"Keep your eyes on me. I'm going to throw the bag at the snake. I will either hit him, scare him, or get him to strike the bag. When I throw, you've got to jump over here to me." Her expression didn't change.

"Nod if you understand," and she did.

"I'm going to count, so get ready, but don't move until the throw."

McGinty kept his voice a whisper as he began. "Three, two, one." and the money bag, weighted by $7,000, flew past Galli's black braided hair and hit the snake. The child's legs had not stiffened in the short time they'd been stopped. She pulled forward with her thin arms as her folded legs scissored up enough to get two feet on the ground, and she hurled her body across the three-foot space she'd kept from McGinty and into his arms. She was unbitten and McGinty watched as the Diamondback uncoiled and moved off into sage, away from its attacker.

Now safe in the arms of a man who'd saved her from a snake, Galli panted, her chest rising and falling in huge breaths as she hugged McGinty. The shared moment stretched time. It could have been ten seconds before they released each other, or had it been ten minutes? But in that short space came McGinty's epiphany. He wouldn't kill the girl, not after saving her life. Finally Galli eased herself back, creating an open space between them. He knew what he had to do.

"Missy, I promised I'd not hurt you and I'm keeping that promise. If I leave you here, can you find your way back to town?"

The child nodded her answer.

"Please wait here a little while to give me more time to get farther away. Please, it's up to you."

Galli kept him fixed with her gaze as McGinty stood and stepped past her. He retrieved the money bag and put it back underneath his shirt. Then he unbuckled his belt, still looped through the straps of the child's overalls. They parted ways as McGinty trudged off into the sea of sage and juniper scrub, trying to extend his one-hour head start on the pursuers who'd surely follow.

* * *

Verrall Black found Samuel Winnemucca stretching and scraping a hide. The mule deer skin was still wet with the moisture of the kill. It had to be dry and tanned before it could be made into gloves for the locals.

"Hello, Samuel, we need to talk."

Samuel was silent as he listened to his neighbor, one of the few whites that he trusted.

36

"Galli's gone missing."

Hearing those three words, the Paiute hunter put down his scraping tool and backed away from his work.

"A bunch of kids were playing hide-and-seek. She hid and the kids haven't been able to find her." Verrall Black waited for a reaction. None came. "They tell me they've looked all over. It's been a little more than an hour." Another pause as both men eyed one another. "She may have fallen asleep, but we don't want to take any chances. I'm going over to ring the school bell and organize a search."

Black turned and as he did, Samuel called back to his wife, inside their wickiup. Pam didn't make any response to what her husband said in their native tongue. She came to their door, stood there with her husband's blanket coat in hand, and stared at the two men.

Samuel took the striped wool coat from her. "Let's go."

The two fathers walked up the dirt street, past the mercantile and the Post Office. The schoolhouse was at the northeast edge of town, alongside the Western Pacific tracks.

The door was open. Nellie Clayton, the teacher, became the janitor on weekends. A cloud of dust flew from the open door. Samuel and Verrall stopped outside and called.

"Ms. Clayton, hello in there, it's Verrall Black, Doris and Melba's Father." The dust began to settle and Nellie came into view in the doorway. She wore a calico full-length apron and her brown hair was tied back with a bandana. She greeted the two men with a simple "Hello," and waited for them to explain their visit.

"Samuel's daughter has gone missing. She's been gone for a little over an hour. I'd like to have the school bell rung, so we can get together a search."

Nellie Clayton avoided making any response such as 'Oh that's terrible.' "I'll ring the bell right now, Mr. Black. Let me know what else I can do." She disappeared from the doorway and soon the clang of the school bell rang out. The ringing of the bell was known to the entire town as a universal signal. The calamity might be a fire, flood or a mountain lion seen lurking nearby. Every man came to the sound of the bell, day or night.

* * *

Two dusty streets away, Charlie Lewis, who'd taken over the mail wagon job after Fred Searcy's death, was doing his regular Saturday chores. His ten-horse team was fed and he had checked every hoof on each horse. Good draft horses were valuable and deserved constant care. The teamster had just stepped under the shed roof and up to the wagon seat using a wheel spoke as a step. He'd check the hand brake mechanism and the leather on his shotgun cradle. Was his lap robe still folded up and ready for his use on the next frosty April morning in the high desert?

When he looked into the wagon box, the shapes and sparkles of silver coins caught his eye. Temporarily rooted to his spot by what he saw, Charlie studied the wagon box floor. There had to be hundreds of dollars lying there. He could also see the section of floorboard that lay next to the coins and the open spot where it belonged. Stepping over the seat and into the wagon box, he leaned forward and looked down into the opening where the floorboard belonged. He ought to see the shed floor, but instead he was looking at a black space. Charlie was just about to investigate further when the school bell rang out. The money and wagon box mystery could wait.

Everett McDermott arrived, and his brothers Dennis and Andrew showed up together, as did Bill and Ed Smiley, Verrall's cousins. Within five minutes, 40 men congregated in the school yard, with more men and women arriving by the minute.

Everett McDermott had already heard from his boys, who'd been in the game of hide-and-seek. Word of the missing child circulated through the group. When Verrall

Black judged a sufficient number had arrived, he issued directions from where he stood on the school house steps.

Charlie Lewis walked the short two blocks over and stood in the school yard. When he learned about the missing child, pieces of information came together in his mind. His wagon was the very one robbed outside Jarbidge. The payroll money had not turned up. Three hundred dollars of the missing loot was in coins. Now there were coins in his wagon and children playing hide-and-seek.

Had Galli accidentally discovered the hidden loot? Who knew where the loot was cached? Only the robbers. *What the hell was the name of the guy who turned State's evidence?* Charlie put the pieces together the only way they seemed to fit. He walked over to Verrall Black and a small queue of citizens.

"Mr. Black, I've got an idea of what's going on here," and he retold what he'd seen and what he believed had happened. "I think that the fella from the mail wagon robbery came back for his money and the girl was unlucky enough to have stumbled across his cache. I bet he's got her."

Verrall, Samuel and the other four men listened in silence to Charlie's theory. "What was the name of that guy anyway who testified against his partners?"

"Bill McGinty," one of the other seven replied.

"And he's out?" asked another.

"Yup," was the reply.

Verrall Black nudged Dennis to get his attention. "Let me get some things going first; searches around town, just in case. I'll get everybody to looking and then the six of us will go over to Lewis's wagon shed."

Verrall Black pointed to specific men to search in different directions, different places. Nothing would be overlooked. Every shed was to be checked. The reeds on the river and creek banks were to be combed and the waters looked at and prodded if necessary. Samuel would have some of his people check on and around the sacred top of Indian Hill. Two Union Cattle Company men would check the cattle corral and loading chute.

Feeling that he'd set in motion a thorough search of the area, Verrall Black closed with a last instruction. "Okay, let's go find the girl." And the groups departed.

"Mr. Lewis, I think we should look at your freight wagon," said Dennis McDermott. The remaining men followed Charlie Lewis back to the wagon shed.

One by one the six men looked at Charlie's discovery inside his freight wagon. Opposite the loose board, the torn cloth coin sacks lay in a pile in the corner of the wagon box. Verrall asked Everett McDermott if he'd mind fetching a gallon bucket from the mercantile. They counted the coins as they dropped into the galvanized bucket; $280 came out of the secret stash.

Verrall climbed up into the box, knelt down, and examined the hidden compartment. He ran his hand over all its surfaces, finding nothing more.

"Searcy was the driver before Charlie took over. That gave him plenty of time to fix this trap in the wagon box. That's how the gang got the loot out undetected!" What they saw squared with what Verrall said. The other men continued to listen.

"Galli is hiding in the wagon box. Somehow she discovers the money. McGinty comes back for the stolen cash. He's not even thinking about kids. But there she is. Now she's already found the money and if he doesn't act now, she'll call her folks and the loot's gone for good. He can't wait and he can't get the money unless he deals with the girl."

"By damn, we're lucky he didn't take a mind to kill her." Ed Smiley shook his head at this possibility and looked for Galli's father, but the Paiute hunter had slipped away from the small group. "Samuel's gone."

Samuel had seen all he needed. He knew what had to be done, and now there was a starting point. He slipped out the

40

back of the shed, the way McGinty would have gone. Tracking the kidnapper and his daughter would be complicated by the footprints that searchers were putting down. The tracks of Galli's playmates and the parties of adult searchers were being added to the kidnapper's trail. He had to find McGinty's route out of town now, before it was lost amid prints from child and adult searchers.

And there it was, two sets of prints, one big and one small, leading northwest toward the Humboldt Mountains. Winnemucca studied the kidnapper's boot print, since he didn't know his face. Any lone white man he encountered would literally live or die by the size and shape of his boot. He had one stop to make before starting out. He went back to his wickiup at the edge of town. His message to his wife was brief.

"She's been taken. I'm going to get her back." Pam put together a knapsack: jerky, matches, gloves, clothes, shoes for Galli and cloth strips for bandages. He added a sharpening stone for the skinning knife that always hung from his belt. He slung his lever-action Winchester rifle over his shoulder. Finally, a ceramic water flask, its cork stopper pressed down hard, dropped into the sack.

"If anyone asks you, tell them I'm hunting." Pamahas stayed silent. "If Mr. Black asks, tell him I'm going to get her back. Tell him please, don't come after me." With his face and dark eyes betraying nothing, Samuel Winnemucca tugged a wide-brimmed, felt hat low onto his head. Then he turned and left the Paiute camp, a man hunter now.

* * *

Back at the wagon shed the talk was about what they should do now. Among the group of five were a shop keeper, railroad men and ranchers. Most hunted, but none were trackers. Sure, they all could follow deer tracks in the fallen snow, but they might not be the best men for the job at hand. When the talk began getting circular, it was time to do

41

something. Doing nothing wasn't an option in Verrall Black's mind. Men didn't stand around wringing their hands and flapping their gums. They acted. His ad hoc leadership unchallenged, Black focused the group and assigned tasks.

"Dennis, get over to the train stations and have them telegraph up and down their lines about the missing girl and McGinty. Ask Oliver to call the sheriff and tell them what we found."

The younger McDermott signaled his understanding and set off for the Southern and Western Pacific depots.

Verrall turned to the new teamster. "Charlie, tell the postmaster about the coins in the wagon box. Then you put a tarp on the wagon, in case the law needs to see or do something with it. I'm going to guess you should find another wagon for your next trip, if the law hasn't been here yet."

"We all have horses and rifles. We need to gather some more men, all mounted and armed. Most of all, we need a tracker. We can all follow deer tracks in the snow or a blood trail but this job's going to be something else. We need men who can track. Do you have any ideas about who we could get? "

The Smiley brothers and Everett McDermott had no disagreement with Black's stepping up to lead or to his directions. No one disagreed because Verrall would be at the head of the posse, the most dangerous spot. They tossed names back and forth. Finally Black put up his hands, signaling it was time to decide and move.

"I'm going to find Wilson Finch, supervisor for the Union Cattle Company. That's our best pool of men. They all have horses and guns. If Wilson can help with a tracker we'll get started. But we'll get moving regardless. McGinty is getting farther away as we speak, and the little girl is at risk."

He turned to the others. "Bill, you and Ed make your way around to all our search groups. Tell em' what we found in Charlie's shed and that I'm getting together a posse. If anyone wants to come along, tell em' to meet up at the school house and wait for me."

* * *

It was three hours after Galli was taken when she made her way back to town. As she came closer, she no longer had to rely on backtracking McGinty's escape route. She picked up her trot to a run and cut across country for home, just missing her father, who had started tracking from the wagon shed.

Pamahas sat outside their wickiup on one of the pine log sections that served as seats around the rock-rimmed fire ring. The mother's eyes were still dry. There would be enough time for tears later, if her fears came true.

Galli called out to her mother in Paiute. Mother and daughter ran into each other's arms. A mother's joy was no different for an Indian mother than a white. Pamahas's eyes filled with tears of relief and joy. Lost in her mother's arms and covered with both kisses and tears, Galli raised her chin to see the weeping face above. Only when both mother and child knew they were truly together did Pamahas release her enfolding arms and hold Galli at arm's length.

Pamahas's questions came simultaneously with her visual inspection. "Did he hurt you?" The child told about the knife point stuck in her knee and pointed to the bloodstain on the leg of her overalls. The small piercing had continued to bleed for many minutes. The combination of Galli's adrenalin and being forced to trot off into the sage had kept her heart pounding.

"Did he touch you there?" Pamahas had already helped her daughter through the first blooming of her body. Galli understood the question and shook her head, "No." The answer brought on another hug from her mother. "Come inside" Pamahas said and led her daughter into their wickiup.

43

"Show me your knee, daughter." Standing in front of her mother, Galli unbuttoned the shoulder straps of her bib overalls and lowered the one-piece garment to the hard-packed dirt floor. Pamahas inspected her daughter. Neither dried blood nor the first tint of bruises marred Galli's olive skin. The girl was untouched. Pam was reassured now; her child was intact and Galli had not just kept silent for fear of revealing abuse. Pamahas's focus moved to Galli's right knee. The small puncture had already scabbed over. She gestured for Galli to redress.

"If your knee bleeds, we'll wrap it, but it's fine for now." Then she asked, "How did he get you?"

Instead of starting at the beginning, Galli began telling about the big snake. Even before the flood of words from her daughter's mouth slowed, Pamahas interrupted, realizing a more immediate need.

"Your father has gone after you and the whole town is searching. We need to let them all know you are back and safe. We'll go to Mrs. Black's house and you'll stay there until your father or I come for you."

Galli listened silently, not yet understanding how wheels already in motion needed to be stopped. As they walked into Deeth and down the three blocks to Libby Black's, Galli resumed narrating the sequence of her unplanned adventure. She described how McGinty hit the rattler with his money bag. Then she delivered her most telling five words.

"Then he let me go."

* * *

Melba and Doris were moping around under the cover of their front porch. Something just less than scowls bent their lip lines to more than normal frowns. Like all the children in town, they were quarantined to the house. A robber-kidnapper was still loose. Libby Black had yielded to her daughter's protests and extended their boundary from within the house itself to the front porch. Melba was the first to see Pamahas and Galli approaching. "Look-look-look!" She pointed, then ran into the house to tell her mother.

"Momma, she's back! Galli and her Mom are here. Come see!"

Leaving the laundry tub and scrub board, Libby followed her daughter back to the front porch. She dried her hands on her apron as they briskly moved through the house.

The Paiute mother and child were two steps away from the wooden stairs from the dirt street up to the porch level. Galli released her mother's hand and ran the final few steps to her pal, Doris. Pamahas Winnemucca stopped at the foot of the stairs. Melba shoved open the screen door to the parlor. It swung wide, stopped only by its coiled retainer spring. Libby grasped the door frame with her hand as she took in the scene; Galli in a reunion with Libby's daughter and Pamahas standing just below. *My God, she's got to be relieved*, Libby thought. Stepping down from the porch, she hugged the other mother. Pamahas made eye contact.

"Can you tell your husband to call off the search? I must tell Samuel. The man released our daughter," pausing, "and she's unharmed." Libby moved her hands from their enfolding hug to grasp Pamahas's upper arms, and spoke.

"Where is Samuel?"

"He is hunting." No clarification was needed. Libby nodded and her gaze moved from her counterpart's face to the school yard far in the distance.

"If you stay here with our girls, I'll find Verrall and tell him." With a confirming nod, she released Pamahas's arms and strode off towards the schoolyard rally point.

As Libby walked towards the school, she spoke to everyone she met and delivered the same message. "Galli is back, safe and unhurt. Have you seen my husband?" She saw Bill Smiley, her husband's cousin, as he headed out of town pursuing his assigned task.

"Bill, the Winnemucca girl is back. He let her go. I need to find Verrall and Samuel."

"I left Verrall at the mail wagon shed, not five minutes ago. I'll go with you," and Smiley turned to lead on, retracing his short path from the wagon shed.

Verrall came into sight as he turned at the corner enroute to the Union Cattle Company Office where he hoped to find Wilson Finch catching up on paperwork at his desk. Libby Black ran ahead as she called out. He turned at the sound of his name.

"Galli's back home. He let her go, and she's at our place. Pam is watching the kids." The words brought forth a sigh of relief. As Bill Smiley approached, she spoke directly to her husband's ear; words for him alone. "Samuel is hunting him. He doesn't know. We have to find him."

His first thought was, *Let Samuel hunt down the son-of-a-bitch.* What had not been done to the girl didn't erase what McGinty had done already. Verrall Black didn't care that McGinty had turned State's Evidence to help convict his crime partners. Mere expedience.

Libby Black read her husband's face, and seeing no softening to the grim set of his jaw, she repeated; "He let her go," and after a moment, punctuated this small bit of redemption. "Unharmed." This time, she noticed a change in his face and an easing of his rigid torso as her words registered. Then Verrall was momentarily silent, thinking about how to respond to the altered situation.

"Libby, you go to the school house and tell Ms. Clayton to ring the bell to recall our searchers. When everyone is back, I want you to tell them the girl is back safe and they should all go home with my thanks. Tell them I'm rounding up a posse to track the kidnapper and any man with a horse and a rifle is welcome to meet me back here, at the school yard." Verrall kissed his wife once and spoke as he parted. "Can you do that for me darling?" His bride confirmed with a quick nod.

They went their separate ways. Bill Smiley moved with Libby to the school yard and Verrall continued to the cattle company office. Sure enough, he found Wilson Finch with his feet up on a scarred oak desk. Two of his veteran cowboys, Virgil Comstock and Shorty Roberts, were sitting on either flank of their boss's desk.

Virgil and Shorty were still in their dusty denim pants and chambray shirts. Their only concessions to being indoors and at the boss's desk were to remove their hats and keep spurred boots off the furniture. All three mustachioed faces turned toward the door when Black entered.

"Hello Verrall. Coffee's still hot if you can manage a cup. Virgil made it, but you can drink it anyway." The cowboys nodded and smiled, their wind-burned faces turned to Verrall in the doorway.

"Wilson, I need a tracker," and he launched into a summary of the day's events. At the telling, the three cut glances to their companions, but only Wilson Finch spoke up.

"We didn't know, by God. We just got back into town not thirty minutes ago from out past Starr Valley. We were up Snow Creek Canyon rounding up strays."

Shorty was usually the silent member of the group. His bushy mustache concealed the imperfection of his harelip. His few words mostly sounded like they began with 'N'. None of his friends took notice of his speech. Shorty was friendly, helpful and generous by nature. He was also the best pistol shot in the outfit. Even at five foot, four inches tall, he was quick to return an insult with a punch, so no one made fun of Shorty.

Virgil Comstock was the polar opposite of his friend, at least in appearance. He stood six foot four alongside his five-foot-four-inch partner, earning the pair the 'Mutt and Jeff' moniker, after their namesake cartoon characters.

After a pause, Shorty ran a leathery palm over his balding head and asked, "Nand snhe's nall nwight...nunharmed?"

47

Verrall's reply was a simple, "Yup," and he repeated his request, now with the backing of today's events.

"Samuel Winnemucca is out there, probably chasing McGinty. We need to help him, because it's the right thing to do," and after a moment, "and keep him from taking the law into his own hands."

Verrall shrugged and turned to the boss. "Wilson, if I recall you scouted for the army in the Bannock War. Do I remember right?"

Finch confirmed his experience.

"Think you can still smell out a trail?"

Again Wilson Finch answered without hesitation. "Verrall, that was over 30 years ago. I'm too God damn old now. But Shorty here is a fine tracker," and Finch gestured towards Roberts. "What about it, Shorty? Are you up for a little tracking?"

"Snure" came the cowboy's answer.

Virgil Comstock then spoke up. "See, we're a package deal; me and him. When and where do you want us?"

Black nodded. "We'll meet at the school yard. Bring bedrolls and some kit. We may be on the trail for a day or so. I'll grab some things from my store. I've already sent word to Oliver at the depot to telegraph up and down the line and phone to let the Sheriff know about the girl and that we're out looking."

"Verrall, one thing, and don't take this the wrong way. But you're damn near deaf. Everybody knows that and it's not a problem here in town. Out on the trail of an armed desperado, that could get you killed."

The bout of scarlet fever he'd suffered as a boy had left Black hard of hearing.

"I know you. You never ask anyone to put themselves at risk when you're not there sharing the risk."

Verrall Black stood alone with his thoughts in the doorway. Finally he spoke a response.

"I'll do the looking and I'll leave it to these two to do the listening."

"Good enough then. I'll send a man to visit all our sheep camps and tell the Basque herders to keep an eye out for this hombre," replied Finch.

Black turned and walked towards his store.

"Nand nwee vetter nget nmoving."

* * *

Virgil and Shorty were not the first arrivals at the schoolyard assembly point. The two Union Cattle Company men joined the other seven already there. Everyone was mounted and armed. Verrall Black came into view where the dirt street entered the schoolyard. He'd brought supplies: coffee, salt, bacon, beans and bullets, which he distributed to the posse.

"Fellas, I'm going to lead the posse. Does anyone have any problem with following me?" When no objections came, Verrall continued.

"It's getting' on to three o'clock, so we've got about three more hours of good light. I'm going out front. I sure hope I can still read trail signs, but I guess we'll find out pretty quick. Now, do you all know each other already?" A chorus of nods, "yups" and "sures" answered back.

"Remember that Samuel Winnemucca is already out there tracking McGinty on his own. He doesn't know that his child's safe at home. So be dang sure of what you see and don't be shooting at anything that moves in the brush. It might be Sam. And try your best to stay quiet."

"All right, Virgil and Shorty are going to flank out to our sides. Charlie Lewis, you ride up with me. Randolph, you ride with Chester. You brothers will ride together and everybody sing out if we pass something you think I missed." Verrall Black let the pairings and directions sink in before he continued.

"All right, we're starting out behind the wagon shed because that's the way McGinty lit out with the child." Verrall reined his horse's head left and with a trot, started out on their quest, leaving the dusty schoolyard empty.

6. The Hunt

Bill McGinty needed every minute of his two-hour lead on any pursuers. There would be a posse. How soon they would be on the trail was the only unknown. He needed all the distance he could manage to have any real chance of getting away.

After releasing the Indian girl, he resumed his pace, trotting back through the sage and scrub junipers. As he reached the edge of the first pines, his cold camp came into view. McGinty had left a newly stolen horse hobbled amid the cottonwoods and alders along the bank of Tabor Creek, which fed into the Mary's River. The bay gelding cast an indifferent eye on its newest master and loosed a stream of piss onto a flat rock beneath its feet.

Time was precious, and McGinty made quick work of breaking camp. Saddles were harder to steal than horses, even from an isolated ranch. His only possession was a bedroll that had come with him from Elko. He folded it double as a makeshift saddle blanket. His mind went over the future after his escape. *Three days, maybe four and I'll be in Mexico and beyond the reach of Nevada law. The money under my shirt will put me in tall cotton from here on.*

From atop of his mount, he checked the site. He'd left not even a dead camp fire to mark the spot. He'd be gone before anybody followed his foot trail back this far. He planned to double back east and head for the newly established border town of Wendover, Utah, and then on to Salt Lake City. There he'd try to hop a train to Tucson before making his way into Mexico.

I'll be a thousand miles away before the law knows I'm out of Nevada.

He could keep his stolen horse, avoiding towns in the wilds of Utah and Arizona. He would stay in the back country if he saw too many lawmen circling around when he got to Salt Lake City.

As he moved along Tabor Creek, the cottonwoods and alders offered ready cover, if he needed to hide from any approaching law. His approach roused mule deer from their beds along the creek. Three miles farther on, the confluence of Tabor Creek and the Mary's River came into view.

He heard the rush of the river, swollen now to its high-water point by the late April snow melt from the heights of Jarbidge Canyon. When he'd seen the river before, it was seldom more than a twenty-foot width of narrow cascades that ran between its many boulders. The water, always clear but quiet then, was now replaced by torrents that covered the boulders.

The afternoon light would soon fade. He needed to get across the river today. The crossing denied any pursuers a clear track to follow. They would need to do a wide search because he might have stayed in the river for a ways upstream or downstream. The posse couldn't move farther until they were sure.

McGinty surveyed the bank, seeking the best place to cross this last obstacle in his path to the Utah line. He chose a likely spot not too far downstream, where the thick stands of cottonwoods allowed him in and out on the far bank. In he rode, urging his reluctant mount into the cold, unknown depths of the rushing water. He could only guess at the depth of the river or the footing in the riverbed below. Six feet out into the river, with another fifteen feet to go, the water was up to his mid-thigh and shoulder level on the horse.

Forty feet upstream a log, long in the water, was dislodged by the force of the cascading snow melt. It lurked just below the surface, riding the spring torrent down from the mountains. Cresting the submerged boulders, it rammed into horse and rider. McGinty's leg, already numbing from the icy water, didn't even immediately register pain as the eighteen feet of wood struck his hip. The improvised saddle disappeared when he was knocked from his horse.

The stolen horse, shielded from the log's impact that tore McGinty's skin and broke his bones, was knocked over onto its side. The animal thrashed and kicked as it tried to keep its head above water in a desperate swim to the far shore.

As the log plowed over McGinty's side, dagger-sharp wood points tore his jacket, shirt and flesh with equally deadly force. Still awake when he went under the water, he struggled to pull himself to shore using his one unbroken arm. His shattered leg, hip and arm sank beneath him. The current fought to keep him in its grip and away from the banks. Shock and cold prevented him from feeling the warm blood fanning out in a crimson plume behind his body. Fighting the river sped his blood loss. Soon his mind drifted from gray to black. He didn't even feel the burn of trying to draw one more breath and getting only water.

As the horse reached the far shore, McGinty's body lodged between two boulders at a river bend. The leather moneybag from inside his shirt stayed pinned to one of the deadly wooden spikes that had ripped the thief. The bag rode on downstream. It finally came to rest, still stuck on the log with other wood debris deposited on the banks of the Mary's River.

* * *

Samuel Winnemucca moved fast on foot, leading his horse, which might be needed later to pack out a body. For now, nothing was more important to Samuel than correctly reading the signs left by McGinty and Galli. Knowing where the trail began, out back of the wagon shed, gave him his crucial starting point.

Just like with the four-legged quarry he'd tracked for years, moving slowly enough to recognize every footprint or broken twig was necessary. Losing the trail or taking a false path kept his daughter at risk that much longer. Reading the trail right was more important than trying to read it fast. Curiously, the child's tracks appeared to travel in both directions. He had no explanation. An escape perhaps, but the tracks back towards town were regular and not blurred like a runner would have left. Confronted with this mystery, he searched on and hoped the trail would soon explain itself.

Two hours on the trail put him three miles from town. There he found signs that his quarry had stopped. The ground told a story. Small feet had been stumbling before their respite. The prints said that man and child sat down on opposite sides of the dirt trail, according to the mark of thighs on the ground. Inside the center of the smaller impression, liquid showed in a small circle. The dirt beneath was still damp as he knelt and smelled the dark patch. Urine.

Something had frightened the child and she'd involuntarily wet herself. This was not Galli answering nature's call. She'd been seated and this suggested a great fear on her part. The sandy soil two feet behind her told its story. The snake had been big, according to the width of its coiled circle and the size of its undulating track off into the high sage. A Diamondback rattlesnake had been there.

Something blurred the snake's print until its undulating retreat returned to a familiar pattern. The moccasin print from under Galli's seat was also blurred, but away from the snake, toward her captor. The tableau at his feet said McGinty had somehow warded off the big reptile. Galli had gotten out of its striking range in one quick shuffling leap. The two figures had combined into one print, for a while. Then the child had moved away to a new spot, away from the man and the snake's path in retreat.

Samuel changed his focus to the trail ahead of his own route. McGinty had continued alone. The why of what he saw was unknown. But to his experienced eye, the story was now revealed.

McGinty needed to rest the child when she began stumbling and the coiled rattler was behind her back. Some action, what exactly still unknown, had allowed Galli to scoot to safety. Then captor and captive had parted ways. She headed back to town and he continued his escape. Samuel reconsidered his plan for McGinty. All along his search path to where he stood now, his mind focused on how the edge of his skinning knife would mark the monster forever.

McGinty should live a long life, visibly marked for the world to see. I'll 'cape' the kidnapper like a deer head for mounting on a wall. First I'll render him unconscious, lest the pain to come stops his heart. I'll only need shallow cuts to the skin around the base and back of his neck up to the middle of his scalp. Just like deer hide, his face will peel off with only a few last cuts around the ears and lips. Living for years as a grinning skull will be his reward.

Putting aside all thoughts of revenge for the moment, Samuel headed back down his child's path, praying that she had made her way home safely.

* * *

Verrall and his posse met Samuel not long after their departure from Deeth. Verrall and Charlie, in the lead, saw him riding back towards town. Samuel traveled slow, still watching Galli's trail. Even when her track disappeared, he remained vigilant in case it reemerged. Black raised his right arm high above his head, signaling the posse to halt. "Sam, Galli's home safe. We're going after McGinty."

Although his face revealed nothing, the Paiute's inner self relaxed at the news of his daughter's safe return.

"Pam and Galli are with Libby."

Samuel signaled his understanding.

"Did you see anything that will help us track this bastard?"

Bringing his mount close to Black, he shared what he'd seen and how far ahead he'd gone before turning back. As the two men talked, Samuel's observations passed around between the posse members. With what little he'd learned now in the hands of the posse, Samuel rode the remaining distance into town. His destination was the Blacks' house.

The three girls sitting side by side filled the glider swing seat on the front porch. Galli ran off the porch the moment she saw her father riding up. Melba, assuming the leadership prerogatives of the oldest sibling, issued an order to Doris. "Go tell Mom that Mr. Winnemucca is here."

Even before dismounting, Samuel appraised his daughter's appearance for signs of trauma. His barefoot child smiled up at him. Her face was clean, and she wore a fresh dress that Libby had taken from Melba's wardrobe. Her first stop after arriving with her mother had been into a bath. Her dusty, soiled overalls and homemade flannel shirt went to a wash tub for now.

By the time her father had dismounted and tied his horse to the porch railing, Pamahas and Libby had appeared in the front doorway. Galli kept silent as he approached, unsure if somehow her own doing might have caused the dark event.

Reading the look of concern on his daughter's face, Samuel smiled. Kneeling down, he pulled her into his arms, speaking softly. "You did nothing wrong." Then he asked if the bad man had hurt her.

Shaking her head, Galli lifted the hem of her borrowed dress and pointed to the minor wound on her right knee.

Pamahas joined the two. She put one arm around her husband and the other around her daughter's shoulders and the parents spoke quietly in Paiute.

Libby shared with Pamahas and Samuel what she knew about how Galli's discovery of the mail robbery loot had led to her kidnapping.

Satisfied that the child was unhurt, Samuel spoke aloud to his family and to the Blacks who waited respectfully away from their porch.

"I'm going back to the hunt with Verrall."

The other adults said nothing. Libby understood that Samuel needed to return to the posse. Pamahas knew that his course was not open to discussion.

He remounted and turned the horse back towards the mail shed. Pamahas and Galli went back inside to share the normalcy of food and friends. The pair would stay with the Blacks and not return to their wickiup until the fugitive McGinty was captured or killed.

* * *

Daylight was fading when Samuel turned his horse towards the trail. No longer held to a slow pace, he found Verrall Black and his posse stopped for the night two miles beyond the spot of his daughter's release. Samuel believed a scout like Shorty Roberts would post sentries outside his camp. Pursuing an armed quarry, Shorty was too savvy to let the hunters become the hunted.

Virgil and Shorty were men who'd slept on the ground around their own campfires many times. Their fire was small, made with dry wood so that neither smoke nor flame would alert their quarry. For like reason, Samuel would not shout out to the camp or other unintended ears.

It was full dark, and the stars shone bright against the black velvet sky. The snowcapped peaks of the Humboldt range showed in the west under a moonlit sky. With the camp in sight, Samuel searched for a sentry at a solitary post, facing out into the sage. Perhaps another sentry faced the other direction, towards the peaks.

And there he was, alone but vigilant, twenty yards out beyond the fire. Samuel approached slowly, checking the ground before each foot fall. He twisted between the bushes so they remained untouched and silent. When he was ten feet from the dark guardian, the moonlight shone on the sentry's face. It was Shorty.

While still concealed, one shadow among many, Samuel broke the silence. "Shorty Roberts, it's me, Samuel Winnemucca. I'm coming in. Don't shoot me," and he stood but didn't yet move ahead. When a nod of recognition came from Shorty, Samuel slowly came forward.

"Ni finnured youd ve vack." Shorty pointed toward the camp fire, then motioned for Samuel to follow. Eight men stood around the fire, looking out into the dark as Samuel walked in.

Handshakes and pats on the back led into questions about his daughter. Had she been hurt? How had she come to escape? Did she say anything about the money under the wagon bed? Shorty and the other sentry drifted back to the edge of camp, close enough to hear what was said. Eight of the ten posse members were married. Virgil Comstock and Shorty Roberts were the group's only bachelors who'd not shared the experience of fatherhood. Everyone wondered, but no one asked if Galli had been molested. It was not a question to ask her father now, if ever.

Samuel shared what he knew. He told about the small puncture to his daughter's knee and the rattlesnake. How McGinty had let the child go. The why of McGinty's action stood out as a puzzlement to them all. Finally Samuel shared the only thing he knew about the hidden money, which the posse didn't already know. Galli had exclaimed, "I found lots of money, Papa."

Combined with her description of McGinty hitting the diamondback with a leather pouch, this signaled the $7,000 in paper money from the mail wagon robbery was with McGinty. When Samuel finished sharing his conclusion with the others, they exchanged knowing glances. Someone whistled and everybody saw potential for a recovery and reward in their future.

Then the camp settled in for the night. New sentries took their turns out beyond the fire. With the last beans, bacon and coffee consumed, some laid out their bedrolls using saddles as pillows. Samuel stayed by the fire with Verrall, Shorty and Virgil. The plan for tomorrow was discussed and confirmed among the four. Samuel agreed to ride drag. He'd trail behind the group by fifty yards as a rear guard, better to notice anything or anyone who moved after the posse passed.

Verrall didn't give voice to his thought. *I don't want Samuel to be first to McGinty. We need to keep McGinty alive and that might not be Sam's plan.*

* * *

The camp roused at first light. Coffee brewed while horses were saddled and bedrolls stowed. Breakfast would be cold corn dodger biscuits eaten from their saddles. No one complained. The task at hand was not about the abstract concept of justice. Riding through the cold, cloudless morning was about running down a rabid dog that posed a threat to all their families.

They'd been on the move an hour when Verrall Black signaled a halt at the site of McGinty's cold camp. Sensing its importance he studied the ground and creek bank, thick with cottonwoods and alders. There was no sign of a camp. No fire or tracks, but something? Then Virgil's first clue came to his nose. Horse piss! He dismounted and walked to the thick cover along the creek. The scent grew stronger, and there between the trees were the tracks of McGinty's horse.

"He camped here. There's fresh tracks somewhere at the edge of this clearing. Circle out around and find them."

As the men began their search, Black stood his ground, waiting for Samuel Winnemucca to arrive. He needed to be brought into the search so the trail was not lost as they closed on McGinty. When Samuel appeared, Verrall Black signaled him over and shared the discovery.

"If it was me, I'd stay along the creek or in the creek. Washes out my trail and gives me cover to hide. Sam, how about we check along the creek? See what we can see."

Still mounted, Samuel said, "I'll check along the bank."

On foot, Verrall Black found tracks beyond the ground cover of fallen leaves and out to the soil and sand of the high desert. Sure enough, the ground told him that McGinty had stayed in the trees for only a few yards before moving out to the brush line. Black needed to be sure he was picking the right direction. Satisfied that he was literally on the right track, Verrall whistled as loudly as he could. Then he turned to gather his men and resume their hunt.

Two riders crossed the creek and moved downstream. Another man rode along the creek bank across from where Verrall and the main group followed the tracks, ever alert. McGinty's direction was clear.

At the confluence of creek and river, Verrall Black stopped and everyone gathered. Again the search plan was altered to fit what they knew. McGinty had come this way. Black chose to split the group, keeping Samuel as one of his five. "Virgil, you and Shorty take four men across at the first possible ford. We need to find his track on the other side. Over here, I'll follow along this bank. If you find his trail, send one man back across to come find us. Now, if we find his track over this side, I'll do the same."

"Sounds like a plan. Shorty does this sound good to you?"

"Nats phine."

The two groups separated. Virgil and Shorty and their men studied the river bank before them. Was it safe to attempt a crossing here? The usually docile river was moving fast with the waters high from the annual spring run-off.

Shorty took the McDermott brothers and headed downstream, looking for tracks as they went, and searching for a crossing point. Virgil and the Smiley brothers looked upstream. Within sight of where the posse had met the river, Shorty discovered McGinty's track off the bank and into the cold water.

Shorty called out to their group, still visible through the trees. "Nere's nwere ne nent in." Verrall Black told his group to hold in place while he crossed through the trees and met Shorty at the bank. Black read the ground the same way as Roberts had.

This discovery was important, but Shorty was uncomfortable following the track into the water, which was high and moving too fast for his liking. They'd continue looking for a better crossing option. Verrall Black nodded in agreement with the cowboy's decision.

What Virgil and the Smileys were seeing was no better. Because the Mary's River narrowed upstream its spring run-off water was forced higher and faster. They all could plainly see that the river banks were growing ever steeper, and the waters flowed out of a steep granite gorge. With no good reason to continue, Virgil turned his horse back downstream towards Shorty.

With Virgil and the Smiley brothers back, the six men headed downstream, searching for a place to cross the river. Fifty yards down the bank, an opportunity to cross came into view. Virgil led the group into the water and across to the far bank. Once on the far shore, the party split up, Virgil and the Smileys searched upstream while Shorty and the McDermotts checked on downstream.

Virgil and the Smileys rode parallel to each other, with ten feet of gap between them. Bill Smiley, riding furthest from the riverbank, was first to see McGinty's horse. None of the three had discovered a track up from the water. Neither had they seen any other sign of the fugitive. McGinty had controlled the horse with an improvised rope halter he'd found on a fence post. The halter remained, ground-tying the trained cow pony.

The three stopped yards away from the horse whose reaction to strangers was unknown. Chasing a spooked horse was something to avoid. Virgil dismounted and passed his reins to Ed Smiley. McGinty's horse stopped nibbling the forage, snorted twice and took two steps away from the approaching stranger. Virgil spoke to the horse in a smooth, reassuring voice, long practiced on Union Cattle Company mounts. Man and horse made eye contact as Virgil took hold of the halter rope and then put a gentle hand on its cheek.

"We're friends now. I'm going to tie this old boy up and we'll look for McGinty's tracks." They circled out and around from where the horse had stayed. They found no human tracks and were left with a puzzle. When all three men were satisfied, Virgil decided it was best to connect with Shorty and the McDermotts. Once his group was back together, they'd find Verrall and the rest of the posse.

They crossed the river, with McGinty's horse in tow. They knew Verrall's direction of travel. Verrall and his boys had searched as they went. The six were free to move downstream quickly. When the other half of the posse came into view, Virgil signaled ahead by giving a loud whistle. Verrall then whistled his men from the picket line off their search.

The stolen horse suggested more questions than answers. "We found the horse twenty yards into the brush. He was back upstream, close to where we hit the river," announced Virgil.

"No boot tracks?" asked Verrall.

Virgil shook his head.

"We found no tracks on this side either," said Black. With the sun high in the desert sky, the posse circled to a stop. Men walked off to make their water out in the sage. Coffee boiled and bacon sizzled in a cast-iron pan. The group would rest both animals and men while their leader and his lieutenants discussed what to do now.

Verrall, Samuel, Virgil and Shorty leaned on their saddles in a small cluster as the horses grazed. Finally Virgil spoke up.

"Damn strange there being no tracks."

Nods came in reply but no other possibilities were offered.

"The way I see it, McGinty got thrown by the horse; snake maybe. A man would not willingly give up his horse out here."

"It could have been a lion or a bear, off from where we found the horse. That would explain why no boot tracks," was Verrall's thought.

Samuel listened but didn't speak up.

"We'll mount up and search until dark," the posse leader stated. "I damn sure don't want to go back empty handed because we missed something or stopped fifty yards too soon." With that the four spread the word to saddle up and resume their search.

After six more hours in the saddle, on both sides of the river, they had nothing to show for their time. The ground told them nothing more about McGinty. The river continued to hold McGinty's body in its cold grip.

The posse searched until the late April light began to fail. Camped for the night, fire made, food cooking, the four leaders met. Were they looking at their own failure, or had they been outsmarted by the bandit? What they hadn't seen today was a kill site or human remains. The possibility of McGinty having fallen prey to an animal was discarded. The natural world had not yet chosen to reveal its secret. Tomorrow they'd head back to town.

The camp rose late the next morning. No excitement for the chase remained and no joy from a success. All they were bringing back was a mystery. Every man knew they'd be roundly second guessed. They'd not be receiving congratulatory drinks. Instead, heads would turn away and conversations would be muffled when any of them walked into a room. Everyone ate their morning meal in silence.

Shorty collected the tin plates, cups and utensils from the other three leaders. They'd camped near the bank, so he'd wash the sets of gear in the river. Sand would scour the plates and forks. Clean river water provided a rinse.

Shorty carried the small stack through the veil of trees that lined the bank. Always cautious, he rattled his fork against the stack of cups. He didn't want to share the beach with a newly emerged spring bear. But there was no bear to surprise. Instead, Shorty got a different shock.

Bill McGinty's body had come dislodged from its boulder resting place and beached not ten feet from where Shorty broke through the trees. The corpse lay face down in the shallow water, and the damage from the log to his clothes and flesh was not immediately apparent. The positions of his leg and arm on one side were unnatural; both visibly damaged. Shorty set down his load and hurried back to camp.

"NI vound nim." He gave the news first to Verrall and Samuel, who were getting ready for today's ride. Every head turned. Packing and saddling stopped as the men followed Shorty back through the trees. At the river's edge, they stood in a half-circle and watched as Virgil and Shorty worked together to drag the body out of the water, lifting under the armpits. Once it was out of the water, they turned the corpse face up and laid it down. McGinty's head lolled limply on his neck. The morning sun sharpened the fish-belly white of the dead flesh. One by one each posse member came close, examining the rips to chest and abdomen now exposed under tattered clothes. The broken bones in the hip, thigh and arm were apparent.

In twos and threes the men speculated on McGinty's fate. What did his body reveal about his end? Ed Smiley pointed to the gashes on the body. "Big claws ripped him up." The speculation brought forth signs of agreement from a few.

"How did his body get so busted up then?" his brother Bill wondered out loud.

"The way I figure it, a big cat jumps him somewhere near the river and he gets dumped in the water. Now the cat's waiting on the bank and he's bleeding bad. He's got to make it to the other shore, but he passes out from blood loss and drowns."

Samuel Winnemucca knelt and began examining the body as Ed rattled on. "Then the rapids up above must've busted him up."

Verrall joined Samuel at the body. "So what do you see happened here?" When Samuel drew his skinning knife, the posse leader became concerned. *Is he going to scalp him or cut off something, I wonder? I wouldn't blame him if he did.*

Instead Samuel used the knife to make small cuts just above several of the purple bruise dots that mark the edges of the ripped flesh. Opening the skin above each dot, the Paiute dug out dagger-sharp splinters.

"Wood, not a lion, killed him." He passed the splinters over to Verrall Black.

Ed Smiley abruptly shut up as he examined the splinters being passed from hand to hand. Everyone was quiet as each man tried to assemble a new picture from the new clues. Avoiding the focus of the group, Samuel painted a verbal picture for Virgil and Shorty.

"He's crossing. A big widow-maker hits him; rips him up. He drowns and his horse makes it across."

Now the idle speculation about McGinty's death turned to more purposeful speculation. Everett McDermott was first to raise the question. "What happened to the money, then?"

"It weren't with his horse," offered Bill Smiley, who'd been with Virgil when they found the mount and checked the area. "And it ain't with the body. Buried it?"

The four leaders clustered together while other men, individually or in twos, searched the river bank. "Wherever

65

it is, probably in the river somewhere, it's sure as hell gone now," concluded Virgil.

Verrall allowed treasure seekers a full hour to scour the bank before calling them back. McGinty's body got its last ride on his stolen horse as the posse headed back to town.

LEONARD FRISTOE

Deeth, Nevada, now had its own doctor, a retired Army physician from Arizona. With silver and gold still pouring out of the Jarbidge strike, a barber set up shop, a bank came to town and a second saloon opened. The Deeth Mercantile added the town's first hand-cranked gas pump to fuel an ever-increasing number of motor vehicles.

Less than two months after the posse returned with McGinty's body, Elko County established a Sheriff's sub-station in town. Deputies Bill McCabe and Jim Graves, both used to Deeth, willingly signed on to move there.

The town still lacked a newspaper. The Elko Daily Free Press arrived every morning on the Southern Pacific train. A three-column-inch article announced the reward Newton Crumley and the Winfield Bank were posting. A quarter-page notice appeared in the Daily Free Press and also in the papers sold in Boise, Reno, Salt Lake City, Denver and San Francisco. Crumley and the bank were casting a wide net.

$2500—IN GOLD

For the return of payroll money stolen

Jarbidge, NV. December 5, 1915

— NO QUESTIONS ASKED —

Contact: George Gott

Winfield Bank, Elko, NV.

The Daily Free Press used Deputy Bill McCabe as a local conduit for news from Deeth. McCabe received $10 per month, whether or not he had any tips to pass along. The town's second teacher, Ms. Abigail Gobin, served as their stringer in Deeth. Abby wrote literate copy, which she sold by the column inch. Her article concerning McGinty's demise and the continuing mystery of the stolen payroll money had preceded the reward notice.

* * *

Virgil Comstock nursed his beer as Shorty Roberts sat across the barroom table reading the latest Daily Free Press. He reread the reward announcement, folded the paper, and passed it across to Virgil.

"Nirgil, nook nat nis."

Virgil put down his beer and took the paper, focusing on the place Shorty was pointing. He read the notice and acknowledged it with a disinterested "Yup," but when Shorty reached to take the paper back, Virgil's eyes widened, and he put his hand on it, stopping its removal.

He tapped the article. "You and I might make some money from this."

"Nhow's nat?"

"We were there. Hell, you found the body." He paused for a swallow of beer and to formulate plans. "This here notice is going to bring people to town. This is our gold strike. Who better to guide them to the river? To his cold camp. Where he crossed and where we found his body."

Shorty was nodding in agreement.

"Yuh see, the money in a gold strike ain't really in looking for gold. It's in selling shovels and shoes to the miners! We're gonna sell them what they need to get started."

Shorty drank from his own beer while he considered Virgil's idea.

"This can be our own damn gold mine. We'll get the word out about our guide services. Between the bartenders, the whores, the barbershop and the mercantile, we're in business. What do you say—partner?"

Shorty wiped foam from his mustache before replying, "Nokay" and he paused as his own thought emerged to burnish their new enterprise. "Nets nask Namuel noo."

"Damn good idea. City folks think Indians are exotic and Samuel can guide when we can't."

The two friends agreed on what they'd charge for their guiding services. Shorty would square the deal with Wilson Finch and arrange time away from the cattle company when needed. He'd also see if Samuel Winnemucca was agreeable to joining the enterprise. Virgil set about spreading the word, even before the arrival of the first treasure hunter.

And they came.

* * *

Searchers rolled into Deeth in ever-increasing numbers. Samuel Winnemucca joined Virgil and Shorty's guide service. He was not above taking easy money from the white man. How long the rush would last, no one knew. Virgil and Shorty kept working for the Union Cattle Company. Samuel kept hunting deer for saleable meat and hides.

Galli Winnemucca also found an opportunity. She met trains on both rail lines when they stopped in Deeth. She had toasted pine nuts for sale by the bag, eight ounces for twenty-five cents. Galli sold from a wide, shallow woven basket. Small white paper bags of nuts sat in the basket at her feet on the depot platform. Her usual bibbed overalls were replaced with a traditional Paiute dress. From moccasins to a dyed turkey feather protruding from a rawhide headband, she was costumed to look as "Indian" as possible. All the better to sell to travelers passing through from one city to another.

After Galli's success, other children from the village got into the act. Some carried little signs touting their specialty. "See the Robber's Grave! 5 cents." "Indian Fry Bread 5 cents," and, "Tour the Paiute Village 5 cents." Every Indian child posed for pictures, then smiled and extended a hand, palm up.

Six enterprising Paiute boys concocted an "Authentic Paiute Rain Dance." On alternating days it became a Paiute War Dance. Five boys danced in newly made breech cloths and leather headbands at the end of the Southern Pacific Depot platform. Their sixth member approached each gawking traveler and held out a basket for donations. Their dance was as authentic as their dyed turkey feathers.

Treasure maps cropped up for sale, as the feeding frenzy grew. Charlie Lewis, the inheritor of the U. S. Mail contract and the actual mail wagon, posted signs advertising:

SEE THE MAIL WAGON! 10 CENTS

Neither Virgil, Shorty or any of the other posse members were paying for their own drinks since the fortune hunters arrived. Like rainbow chasers everywhere, most of the seekers had left nothing behind to take a chance at finding something.

Occasionally among the arriving hopefuls was a well-funded group. The biggest of these came from the city world of gas lights and indoor plumbing. They arrived in Deeth, well equipped and funded for a long search. Some brought their own horses or mules. Tents abounded as did new expeditionary clothing and as-yet-not-fired guns.

Such groups wanted to go immediately on the hunt. Often someone who'd studied all available information on the robbery believed they'd figured out the mystery and only needed to unearth the money bag.

When approached by any such group, Virgil, Samuel and Shorty discarded their usual rates. They sized up the bunch and then quoted a price according to what they thought the traffic would bear. Some groups wanted to be taken to McGinty's camp, others to his river crossing. Some wanted their guide to stay on after they were told, "The country is still pretty wild. Indians you know, and outlaws that hide out up in the Humboldts. You'll want to be REAL careful."

* * *

Leonard Fristoe came to Deeth with nothing left behind in Reno and the promise of "Something-Anything," holding great appeal. His last dollars bought a shovel and a train ticket from Reno to Deeth.

The July night after his arrival in town, he needed a meal and a road stake for his treasure hunt. He waited until full dark to break into the Deeth Mercantile. *I bet there's money in there, and I know there's food, guns, and bullets.*

Fristoe circled the darkened building, looking for the best way in. He broke a pane of glass on a ground level storeroom window. Inside the mercantile by match light he gathered salt pork, beans, coffee, a rifle, and a box of 30-30 caliber shells. The big steel safe was too tempting a target to ignore. But how could he get the safe open? Fristoe found the dynamite Verrall Black kept for local miners.

Fristoe thought through both crime and escape, as he loaded the stolen rifle and packed the rest of his haul into a flour sack, ready for a quick departure. *Nobody knows me in town yet. No one saw me break in. I blow the safe, grab the money inside and I'm gone. I'll sleep out in the desert tonight and head for Elko tomorrow. I'm clear!*

Fristoe stuck a length of fuse into the two-stick bundle of dynamite he'd tied to the safe's handle, next to the dial. He lit the fuse and then crouched behind a wooden bean barrel in the corner. The two sticks did the job. When the smoke cleared, the safe door hung ajar from one bent hinge. The safe was empty of any money or valuables. Useless, damaged ledger books were all he found.

With no time to waste, Fristoe opened the front door of the store, looked around, and saw no one. He moved north, past the darkened post office and out into the desert night.

The explosion roused Deputies McCabe and Graves, as well as Verrall Black. From his house 100 feet behind the store, the blast was both felt and heard. As soon as he was in trousers and boots, Verrall lit a lantern, tucked a pistol in his pocket and crossed the open ground to the mercantile.

Black stopped at the near side of the building, listening for sounds of an intruder still inside. After a minute, he peeked through the empty window frame and saw no one amid the damage. When he heard steps approaching, Verrall turned the lantern light on himself to be recognized. McCabe and Graves, both partially dressed, lowered their rifles.

"Thief's already gone. He blew open my safe."

"Jim and I will check inside to make sure he's gone. First light tomorrow, we can track him. I'll call Elko and have em' send up some more men," said McCabe. He asked Black to wait outside while the deputies searched the store. Finding no one, they returned to the porch. Jim Graves was shaking his head at the damage he'd seen.

"As soon as you have a list of what's missing, get that over to our office."

Black would be unable to sleep any tonight. He lit the store's gas lamps and began to clean up the mess, making a list of what had been taken as he went along.

* * *

Early the next morning while waiting for help to arrive, McCabe and Graves located Fristoe's track from the store out into the desert sage. Now they had a starting point. They still needed someone familiar with the territory. The deputies were new to town, and their reinforcements from Elko had never been to Deeth. They turned to Wilson Finch at the Union Cattle Company for help.

McCabe found Wilson at his desk in the company office. "I need a scout, someone who knows the area and horses. I've got five deputies, but none of us know the area. As far as we know, the crook is on foot. Horses will help us close on the rascal. Can you help me here?"

"Sure I can. I'd go myself, but the best person for the job is Shorty Roberts, if he agrees. Shorty runs our range northeast of town, where I'm guessing your man fled."

"So where's Shorty? I'll ask him."

"He's over at our corral, working with some new stock. Get yourselves horses and tack. If Shorty agrees to help, let him know that I'm good with that. If Shorty won't go, bring an extra horse back for me."

Bill McCabe knew Shorty from his previous annual trips to town during the Paiute gathering, but he didn't know the cowboy well. When the company horse corral came into sight, there was Shorty, standing in the middle of the corral, running a lassoed horse around the perimeter. The horse was unbroken green stock. It kicked up dust as it circled, all the while jerking against the unfamiliar feel of the rope around its neck.

"Shorty," called Bill, "we're heading out after the fella that blew up the safe at Verrall Black's store. I need someone who knows the ground like you do. Would you be willing to join me?" There was no hesitation between McCabe's question and Shorty's answer.

"Shorty, we need five horses too."

With that, Roberts called out toward the company bunkhouse. A barefoot young cowboy, Karl Schmidt, pulled his suspender straps up onto his shoulders as he emerged from the shadowy bunkhouse into the pale morning light.

"Net snome nelp nand snaddle snix norses." With wheels set in motion, Shorty turned to Bill McCabe. Together, the two men waited outside the corral for Schmidt to return with the mounts.

Cattle company men walked the mounts back to Shorty, who chose his horse and got into the saddle. Bill McCabe took the reins of two horses and mounted up. Shorty told Schmidt to follow them with the other animals. The three men headed back to the mercantile.

Help arrived when Deputies Alvin St. Claire, John Armstrong and Harry Moulton rolled in. With five deputies, horses and a local tracker, they were ready to follow the robber.

Bill McCabe sent his partner Jim Graves to the Deeth Mercantile. Verrall Black handed over the list of things taken; food, a Remington lever-action rifle and cartridges. The stolen rifle caught the attention of both deputies. They'd be tracking an armed man with the ability to shoot from a distance.

Bill McCabe introduced Shorty Roberts to the three Elko deputies. He then shared the bad news that they were tracking an armed man. While it was not a good situation, the five would do what needed to be done because it was their job. Nevada lawmen didn't shrink from danger, nor did Shorty Roberts. But it meant that they would be quicker to shoot.

* * *

Once out of the last two blocks of Deeth, the fugitive could go north, east toward Starr Valley or west into the Humboldt range. None of the deputies were city boys. All had grown up somewhere in Elko County, so tracking game was already in their skill set.

The tracks led off northeast towards the foothills of the Rubies. The six men spread out into a phalanx formation with Shorty at the forward point. Advancing slowly, their spacing ten yards apart, they moved forward through the sage. All eyes scanned ahead and to their flanks, searching for their quarry. Shorty looked only at the boot tracks pressed into the sandy soil. To lose the track was to lose time and distance from their man. On they rode. Their advance was patient and steady.

Leonard Fristoe made it five miles before the moonless night risked too many accidents. He settled down on the bank of a small stream. A busted ankle could be the death of him, figuratively, if not literally. He expected to be pursued by the law. He tried to sleep until first light, but his rest was fitful. Every night sound raised an alarm in his mind, so only the powers of fear and adrenalin fueled his body now. Looking at the bag of stolen food, so near but far from being available without a campfire, only made the morning chill worse. *Well, at least I've got water and a weapon.* These were his only comforts.

When the sun appeared over the Ruby peaks, Fristoe noticed the creek water was stopped by a beaver dam. *Shit, Beaver fever. Drinking from here will guarantee me a gut ache and the drizzlin' shits.* He planned to keep moving. He didn't know where to, but anywhere away from Deeth was enough for now. Getting to his feet, he stretched the stiffness out of legs and back. Then he started out, away from his crime.

The robber had been more concerned with covering distance than with concealing his trail so his track was easy to follow. The horsemen were moving twice the speed of a man on foot, so they soon caught up. Fristoe saw the horsemen before they saw him and he crouched low in the brush hoping to escape notice. The desert gave him the cover of three-foot-high sagebrush, but nothing else. He crouched down and hoped the riders would pass. They didn't.

Deputy St. Claire, riding the right edge of the phalanx, thought he saw something up ahead. Was it movement or a reflection from something metal? He alerted the phalanx and the six riders dismounted and advanced on foot, slower but safer in pursuit of an armed man.

The first shot rang out. St. Claire screamed as the bullet tore into his thigh. Everyone in the posse immediately searched for the target. Who got hit? Will I be next?

John Armstrong, five yards to St. Claire's left, reacted without thinking. "Alvin's hit!" He turned to see where his friend had fallen. Fristoe's second shot hit Armstrong in the shoulder and he went down. The hunters had become the hunted.

"Stay down!" shouted Bill McCabe.

When the second shot erupted, Shorty looked back to see if anyone else had been hit. St. Claire and Armstrong both needed help, but his greatest value would be in silencing the shooter and not trying to staunch the deputies' wounds.

The sound of the shots placed the criminal ahead and to his right. That was all Shorty knew when he began crawling. He reached down to his side and drew the revolver riding on his hip. Whether the three other riders were staying put or trying to help their friends was unknown to him. His job, his only job, was to stop the shooter.

Fristoe saw the two men fall. Killing them all was not his goal. Slowing them enough for him to get away was what he wanted. His pursuers had gone to ground, two wounded and four more dismounted. Had he scared them away? Were they all family men who thought first of their wives and family? He hoped so.

Shorty moved forward, propelled by his elbows and knees, his belly in the dirt and a pistol in his hand. He knew he was close. He had learned to use all his senses out in the desert. He could smell cattle before he saw them. Now he smelled his human quarry. Instead of advancing, Shorty waited for the shooter to make the next move.

Fristoe and Roberts lay only ten feet apart in the desert dust. As the morning warmed, the sage broadcast its distinctive aroma, while both men listened for movements from their enemy. Patience and experience had taught Shorty he had to outlast Fristoe.

Seeing nothing and hearing only distant moans, Fristoe decided to try to slip away. It was the few noises of his rise and first slinking steps that gave Roberts the angle he needed. As Fristoe moved, so did Shorty, closing on his prey.

Shorty saw tiny bits of dust hanging in the air, raised by Fristoe's footfalls. Then he saw the robber's back. Still moving in a low crouch, the target was directly ahead when Shorty aimed and fired. His shot struck Fristoe in the buttocks.

Pain, impact and surprise combined, and Fristoe dropped both his rifle and flour sack of stolen food. "Ahh, shit!"— his scream, unmuffled. Rolling onto his side, Fristoe grabbed his wound. When he looked up, Shorty stood over him, gun pointed and ready to shoot.

"You shot me!"

Shorty nodded. When Fristoe began moving a hand towards the rifle, Shorty re-cocked his pistol and shook his head. "No." The combination of the gesture and the mechanical click of the pistol's hammer rotating the cylinder stopped Fristoe from continuing to reach.

Bill McCabe was at Deputy St. Claire's side. Now he advanced to where Shorty stood, his own pistol drawn. As McCabe looked down at Fristoe, neither of the two were sure if McCabe would fire another bullet into the bandit who'd shot two of his people.

"Stand" commanded McCabe.

"I can't, I'm shot," responded the man on the ground. McCabe's response was instantaneous. His pistol extended towards the robber's chest. "Get up or die where you lie, you son of a bitch."

John Armstrong's gunshot wound to the shoulder was painful but not life threatening. Alvin St. Claire's thigh wound was bleeding badly. A tourniquet stopped the flow. He needed a doctor, and quick, or both his leg and his life were at risk. Armstrong could ride. Fristoe, now in hand-irons, walked. Shorty supervised Bill McCabe in quickly fashioning a sled for Alvin St. Claire who couldn't ride back on his horse.

Leonard Fristoe spent the night in the two-cell Deeth jail house. The next day he traveled, in irons, back to Elko with the three deputies. Within two months, Fristoe was tried and sentenced to 28 years in the Nevada State prison. Shorty

Roberts was a hero. In the weeks that followed, he was recognized by both a congressman and the governor for his bravery. He had saved the lives of two wounded deputies and brought a dangerous criminal to justice.

Joseph Pulitzer's *New York World* newspaper specialized in sensationalism. Scandals, sex, corruption and crime were the paper's stock in trade. One of Pulitzer's junior editors heard about the Jarbidge mail wagon robbery and the reward. With a murder among the thieves, betrayal, kidnapping, and hidden loot all in the mix, this story was worth pursuing. Mr. Pulitzer himself received the pitch.

"Sir, if we send a reporter out there, we can ride this horse for weeks. Daily dispatches from the western front. I think there's gold in this story, boss."

Pulitzer agreed. Reporter Harry Hamlet and photographer Jack Chase were dispatched to Nevada. Pulitzer saw journalistic gold in the Nevada hills. He'd have to order extra barrels of ink for this series.

Their orders were to send back daily reports with pictures. Hamlet was to tell the story of the circle of crimes: Fred Searcy's murder, the robbery, McGinty's betrayal of his fellows, and the kidnapping of the little Indian girl. To milk the piece even further, Hamlet and Chase would pursue the hidden payroll money. The editor gave a final admonition to Hamlet as they departed from the Union Station.

"Don't let things like details get in your way."

* * *

Hamlet and photographer Chase rode 2500 miles west on thinly padded wooden seats. They'd been reminded back in New York City that the paper was financing a story and not a vacation for the two. Both New Yorkers came west in wool suits, brogan shoes, neckties and hats. Only their hats, one a bowler and the other a flat-brimmed straw boater, managed to retain their shape by trip's end.

After three days on the train the Easterners stepped onto the depot platform in Deeth wearing rumpled and sweat-stained clothes. Their neck ties had become polishing cloths for shoes but that practice was quickly discarded. Then the ties fell to even a worse fate as handkerchiefs.

The two strangers emerged from the Pullman coach into the hot August sun. They stood next to their suitcases and Chase's camera gear on the station platform. Before them, Chase and Hamlet saw photographic gold: Galli selling pine nuts. Her competition was seven-year-old Thocmentony Besa-Yoona, Tony for short, who sold her mother's 'Indian Fry Bread.' Down at the end of the platform, five young Paiute boys danced for the passengers emerging from the train.

"Jack, get pictures of the station and especially the Indian kids. We tell our story, my words and your pictures, right from the start." Hamlet's writing had actually begun on the trip west. Just as Mark Twain had done for *Innocents Abroad,*

81

his narrative started with the journey. Hamlet wanted the readers to understand how far the *New York World* would travel to bring them the news.

While Jack Chase captured the charade that spread before them, Harry visited with the Southern Pacific station agent. "Good afternoon." He fanned himself with his straw hat. Compared to the swelter and humidity of New York, the 86 degrees of the Nevada August was almost tolerable.

"Hello," smiled the agent.

"We need to get into town," and he paused, waiting. His smile disappeared when the agent answered.

Raising a forearm from the depot counter, the agent pointed out the door to the collection of buildings lining the dirt street. "That's it."

Not wanting to alienate the first local he'd met, Harry just smiled and kept fanning. "Hotels?"

"Mister, you're in luck, we just got our second hotel, the Silver House. It's just a couple doors up the street from Mrs. Nicely's boarding house. Three blocks thataway," and again his index finger pointed, pistol like, as sufficient directions.

"One more thing, if you can. My associate and I are here from the *New York World* newspaper. We're doing a story about that big robbery, the kidnapping, and all the details. Our readers back east are real interested in such things."

The agent nodded politely, waiting for the question.

"We need to interview the people involved. Mr. Roberts, Mr. Black, Mr. Comstock, and the Indian family, if they'll talk to us. Where might I locate some of these folks?"

The station agent smiled at the sweating stranger. "Shorty Roberts and Virgil Comstock both work for the Union Cattle Company. When you fellas get your rooms, they can tell you how to find the company office. If it's in the evening, try the Cannon; it's a saloon and dance hall. Shorty and Virgil will probably be there."

"Thanks a million," and the reporter extended his right hand in thanks. They shook, and Hamlet turned to go.

"One more thing." The station agent aimed his arm and index finger past Hamlet to Galli Winnemucca and her basket of pine nuts. "That's the girl." Hamlet's eyes widened, and he was about to go, but the station agent spoke first.

"You best talk to her father before you go speaking to an Indian child. Just so you don't get off to a poor start." As he spoke, the agent set his elbow down on the counter and casually drew his index finger horizontally across his neck. Perhaps the gesture meant nothing, but Hamlet didn't want to take the chance. Just out the door, Harry left with a "Thank you," and parted with a quarter to buy a bag of pine nuts from Galli.

* * *

Harry Hamlet and Jack Chase came west with suitcases, camera gear, and polio. Neither man knew healthy people could be asymptomatic disease carriers. Medical science was in a race with the disease and polio had a head start.

Since 1913, polio had been steadily spreading. New York City was the epicenter of an epidemic. In 1916, the city's dead numbered 2,343 or 28.5 cases per 100,000 residents.

City health officials took the unpopular measure of sending the police to forcibly remove children under the age of sixteen from their homes. Children with symptoms of the disease were confined away from unaffected children. The cries and protests of their mothers were ignored. Most were Italian immigrants who clustered in ghettos such as "Pig Town" in the borough of Brooklyn.

White families on Staten Island were somehow overlooked, and the virus marched on. Central to polio's spread were the twin problems of misinformation and lack of information.

Medical science knew polio was principally spread through fecal-oral transmission via water, food, or direct contact. Dirty hands were the culprit. It was obvious to the white community that failure to wash thousands of immigrant hands was a moral failing. Personal health was still untethered from public health. Lack of running water and lack of sewers in Pig Town were not seen as root causes of the epidemic.

Science was just learning that the virus could also be spread, person-to-person, by saliva droplets from a sneeze or cough. Yet to be discovered was how asymptomatic carriers fit into the vortex of disease spread.

By the end of 1916, polio had reached across the nation. New York State was high among states with its six-per-100,000 infection rate. Nevada had the highest infection rate of any state at 9.7 cases per 100,000 people.

Were Harry and Jack to blame? Unintentionally they were part of the problem. With seven to ten days between transmission and the presentation of symptoms, they still were ignorant of their effect on Deeth when they departed.

Like the Italians of Pig Town, the Paiute community was blamed when the epidemic arrived in Nevada. Scientific and medical ignorance hadn't connected public health with personal health. As fate dictates, especially with its handmaidens ignorance and fear, the public was wrong.

Long after polio's arrival in Nevada, scientific research determined that it had been endemic to mankind for centuries. The majority of people acquired an immunity by having had a mild case of the disease during childhood without even knowing it. What changed something endemic into a pandemic was modern sanitation. Humans in cleaner communities often lost their natural immunity to the disease.

When polio escaped through the blood to our nervous systems, it could destroy that system's message-sending ability. Then paralysis followed. Paralyze a limb and you were disabled. Paralyze the chest muscles and you died.

* * *

Once settled in Mrs. Nicely's boarding house, the two carriers ate at the communal table before moving on to the Cannon saloon, where Shorty and Virgil were sharing a table with three other cattle company men.

Heads turned when the visitors entered. Their clothing announced them as city people, even before they spoke. Harry strode to the bar and ordered two Manhattans. Bartender Ed Smiley's look as he stared across the bar was the same as if the stranger had two heads. The Cannon was a beer and whisky saloon. The height of choice was, "Bourbon or rye?"

Smiley set glasses on the bar in front of Hamlet and poured two shots of whisky. "On the house," and he went back to polishing glasses.

"Thanks," said Harry. "Can you tell me if Shorty Roberts is here tonight?"

Smiley turned. Still holding a half-polished glass, he gestured towards five men at a table in the corner. "He's the short fella with the big mustache." Smiley paused before continuing. "Shorty talks a little funny, but you might not want to notice, so your drink don't get spilled."

Jack was still standing by the door, waiting to follow the reporter's lead. With a whisky in each hand, Harry motioned towards one of the empty tables. Jack sat down and received his free drink. "What the hell?"

"Don't ask." Lowering his voice, Harry said, "He's the little fella at the table in the corner. Wait here while I go over and make contact." One step away from their table, Harry turned to Jack, "Get us a couple of beers."

"Excuse me gents…Mr. Roberts." Hamlet paused, waiting for Shorty to acknowledge his presence. All five cattle company men were now regarding Harry. Shorty looked the stranger up and down. Virgil leaned a little closer and without breaking eye contact took another sip of his beer.

"Mr. Roberts, I'm Harry Hamlet. I'm a reporter from the *New York World* newspaper. My editor sent me here because our readers want to hear about the Jarbidge robbery and the posse that tracked that fella McGinty." Harry stood waiting for a response.

The cowboys exchanged looks but none spoke, so Harry waded in again. "Can I buy you fellas another beer?"

"Snure. Mull nup a chair."

Hamlet asked Jack to send over five beers.

Virgil Comstock grinned. Seeing an opportunity, he jumped in. "Forgive my friend. His first language is Norwegian and that nordski accent makes him hard to understand. Isn't that right Oddvar?"

"Niss ny nass Nirgil" and the other four men at the table stifled laughs. But the ice had been broken.

"I'm Virgil Comstock. Shorty and I were in the posse. Shorty here found McGinty's body. Isn't that right, Shorty?"

"Namn snraight"

"What I'd like to do, if it's possible, is get one or both of you to take us," pointing over to Jack Chase, "around to all the places we've heard about. The paper will be glad to pay you for your time."

Virgil held up one finger to pause the conversation. He motioned for Shorty to lean closer. Then he whispered into his friend's ear, "We've got one." Shorty nodded in agreement and sat back in his chair.

Virgil paused for judicious thought. "Well, that's something we'd have to think about. We've not done such as that before. Then there's getting time off from our boss. August is a busy month in the cattle business. You probably already knew that." Virgil banked on the newcomer wouldn't know that he and Shorty were already in the "guides for hire" business.

"This would take some time, you see. What with a trip up to Jarbidge and then following our trail out to the Mary's, we're talking some days here. We'd have to rent horses for you boys. There's food to arrange and gear for you. There are lots of moving parts here." Shorty and the other two cowboys spontaneously offered support. "Yup—Nabsolutely—That's some days all right."

"I'm able to pay $25.00 a day."

Virgil smelled blood in the water. "Each, I assume. I'm guessing you'd want us both, since we were both in the posse?"

Hamlet hesitated at the extra money he'd have to justify to the accountants who knew nothing about reporting or newspapers beyond using them to line bird cage floors.

Everyone watching knew that company horses and gear were a no-cost item. They also knew that Virgil and Shorty guided for $10 a day. Virgil's question hung unanswered over the table.

"I'm sure my editor will agree that I need you both."

"Well, let's do this. Tomorrow, Shorty and I will confer with our boss and see if he can spare us for a few days during our busy season. You check with your people. Oh, you and your friend need to get some traveling clothes over at the mercantile. Levi's, boots, shirts, jackets, and hats."

"Here's to the paper," toasted Virgil as beer mugs lifted from the round tray. "You understand this deal is all cash. Better figure on four days and another $100 for horses, food and sundries." Virgil was on a roll. "That's in advance, you understand."

Hamlet nodded and agreed to meet back at the table tomorrow night. He hid his worry about the editor's response and simply smiled as he departed.

"Virgil, what are sundries?"

"Shut up, Jimmy."

* * *

Hamlet sold his editor on the need for both Comstock and Roberts taking him around. "Boss, I know it's more than you wanted to spend, but I can interview them both while we're on the trail. Jack will get all his pictures at the same time. Those two things alone save you money that you'd have had to spend, so all we're doing is moving money around."

That night at the Cannon saloon, Virgil and Shorty shared the table with Harry and Jack. Attired in stiff new jeans and boots not yet broken in, Harry and Jack believed they fit right in. Of course, they looked like city folks playing at being cowboys.

"My editor almost had a shit hemorrhage, but I convinced him you fellas were the key to the story."

"Our boss was none too happy, but he's letting us take four days off. That's all he can spare us," Virgil informed the two. "I see you got those trail clothes over at Black's place." He kept a poker face. "We'll meet you outside the boarding house at 7:00 A.M. tomorrow. I never asked either of you fellas if you could ride a horse. I guess we'll find out."

* * *

Virgil, seated next to Shorty, spoke from the driver's seat of a company Model T Ford when they met Harry and Jack the next morning. "You'll be glad we're not riding a horse all the way to Jarbidge."

Shorty agreed, "Nyup."

Harry and Jack climbed into the back seat of the sedan.

"I expected to be on horseback today," said Hamlet.

"Jarbidge is too far for us to make on horseback in one day. Believe me, you fellas don't want to make that ride." The back of Shorty's head was visible as he vigorously nodded in agreement with Virgil.

Their first stop was in town, at the wagon shed behind the Post Office. Charlie Lewis agreed to let Virgil and Shorty show the reporter the actual mail wagon from the robbery. As Jack set up his camera, Virgil showed Harry the hidden compartment below the wagon bed. He lifted out the unsecured board.

"The local children were playing hide-and-seek on a Saturday. Galli Winnemucca was hiding in the wagon. She kneeled on the back end of the board, like this," he tipped the wood up by pressing on one end. "and by accident she discovered the hidden robbery money."

"Aha," escaped Harry's lips. "Jack, you need to get a couple of pictures of the wagon bed. Do one shot with the board in place and another with it off, okay?"

The two cowboys stood back and waited until Jack had what they needed. Then it was back in the car.

As the four drove up the dirt road, Virgil filled them in on the sequence of the robbery. He described the capture of the three men. Then he explained how Ben Kuhl was linked to the crime scene and to the murder of Fred Searcy.

Harry Hamlet had a list of questions he needed to ask. He'd ask, listen to the answer, and only then write notes to himself. Some answers raised new questions in his mind. Shorty and Virgil answered all his questions and clarified which were their assumptions and which hard fact.

Once they got up the canyon from the Jarbidge cut-off, Shorty stopped the Model T. Jack Chase took pictures of the river canyon and the winding road. They stopped again at the abandoned miner's cabin where the Kuhl gang hid out and was captured. Shorty helped Chase set up his camera equipment and offered himself as a part of the image.

The four stopped again where the mail wagon first saw the three gunmen. Virgil walked Harry and Jack to the spot where the bandit's horses were hidden. As Virgil answered questions, Shorty and Jack decided on a spot in the dirt road. Jack posed Shorty Roberts kneeling, with an index finger pointing down to an imaginary blood stain. Chase logged the significance of each image into his notebook. 'The spot where driver Fred Searcy died,' would be the caption for this image.

They drove the last miles into Jarbidge. Jack Chase took photographs of the town, including Newt Crumley's saloon and the North Star mine. While Jack worked with Shorty's help, Harry Hamlet and Virgil went to the mine office in search of Clarence Cornwall, who was on the mail wagon when it was robbed. The mine office was closed for the day, so the pair walked back to the next obvious choice, the Success Saloon.

Newt Crumley's saloon was the de facto community center for Jarbidge. Food, drink, female companionship, and Faro were all available. Besides offering relief for all of man's earthly needs, the bar was a repository for all the news. Foreman Cornwall had come and gone already. The company provided the mine foreman with a separate bungalow. He was not in the miners' bunk house.

The day's travel had used up the daylight, so they'd stay the night in Jarbidge. An over-night allowed Hamlet to interview not only Cornwall but also Postmaster Scott Fleming. Harry also hoped to interview Frank Leonard, who'd led the rescue party which found Searcy's body. Leonard was a priority. He'd also led the armed search party who'd found the bandits holed up in the miners cabin they'd seen on the way up the canyon.

Harry Hamlet paid for two rooms upstairs at the Success Saloon. The four ate and drank in the bar that night. Luck was on their side, when Frank Leonard, himself a North Star miner, came in for his nightly drink. The bartender pointed Hamlet's group out to Frank as he drew the miner's beer.

"I understand you fellas wanted to speak to me," asked the tall hard-rock miner. "I'm Frank Leonard."

Both surprised and delighted, Harry Hamlet got up from their table, still littered with empty plates and half full beer mugs. "Mr. Leonard, I'm Harry Hamlet. I'm a reporter for the *New York World* newspaper. I've come to Nevada to share the story of the mail wagon robbery and the kidnapping of the little girl with our readers." Next he introduced his guides and Jack, the photographer. Leonard listened in silence. He was not interested in the New York readers or having his name in print. Frank was interested in two or more beers and something to eat.

"Maybe the paper could buy you a drink and dinner if you've not already eaten?"

Frank Leonard signaled that the paper could buy his dinner.

Pointing to an empty table, Harry excused himself from his group and sat down to interview this key player in his story. "Please order whatever you like."

"Gus, I want steak and beans. Do you still have that bottle of good rye whisky under the bar?"

Gus the bartender said he did. The only bottle of 'Old Overholt' in Jarbidge made its way to their table.

Harry Hamlet got his money's worth. Frank Leonard added details and filled in information that Virgil and Shorty had only heard about. With more notebook pages filled, Hamlet thanked the miner and made one last request. "Would you let Jack take your picture?"

Encouraged by the good rye whisky, Leonard agreed.

Jack Chase photographed Frank Leonard standing at the bar. Above the back-bar mirror, the ornate sign read, "Success Saloon—Jarbidge Nevada." Jack's image showed the brave posse leader and also the setting. His picture would be a worthy companion to Harry's 1,000 words.

That night as usual, Harry Hamlet set down on paper the day's adventure. His words, combined with Chases' imagery, brought the wilds of Nevada to the paper's metropolitan readership. Untethered from the truth when necessary, Harry added imagery and excitement when neither were present in the day's reality. Mark Twain would have been proud of Harry Hamlet's homage to *Innocents Abroad*. It was indeed the sincerest form of flattery.

The next morning, he interviewed Postmaster Scott Fleming. Then he focused on Clarence Cornwall, who was delighted to share every gory detail of the robbery and murder. Clarence pointed out his own personal bravery. Harry had what his editor wanted.

Hamlet wrote titles and tag lines that he'd work into his daily articles. "Robbery in the River Canyon" — "Murder in the Nevada Snow" — "The Mail Wagon Murder." Heading back to Deeth, Harry asked for more local stories. Maybe these tales about the still-wild west, true or not, would burnish his career back East.

The Ford made it to Deeth before dark and suffered only one flat tire enroute. The four met for dinner at the new hotel two hours later, where Shorty and Virgil previewed tomorrow's ride, starting at the wagon shed and continuing to McGinty's cold camp and beyond. Harry and Jack were told to be outside at 7 A.M. tomorrow, ready to ride.

* * *

In the morning, four company horses were saddled and waiting outside the boarding house. Shorty had ordered up his and Virgil's favorite mounts and two docile mares for the city boys. "Well, let's go, fellas." Both cowboys suppressed laughs when Harry, with one foot in the stirrup, lost his balance and fell over backwards. "Grab the saddle horn next time," said Virgil.

"The what?"

"The thing sticking up on the front of the saddle there." Virgil and Shorty had agreed that not discouraging the newspaper men was important. Who knew where the New York news story might lead? The world always needs new heroes. Who better to be the next movie star, like Tom Mix.

Harry stayed up on his second try. With Jack also in the saddle, Virgil secured the camera tripod behind the photographer. They passed a few basic instructions for steering and stopping their mounts. Virgil took the front with Harry riding at his side. Shorty followed with Jack riding herd on him.

The newspaper men were passengers more than riders. Shorty and Virgil stayed near them, and the two mares were followers, not leaders. Starting at the mail wagon shed, they followed McGinty's trail into the desert. Virgil showed where the tracks crossed the rail line and entered the brush on the opposite side.

Shorty had specific landmarks in his memory for a spot where Galli's encounter with the rattlesnake probably took place. He retold the story: the stop, the snake, the rescue, and the release, as he'd heard it from Galli's father.

Harry asked for a stop so Jack could photograph the spot. "But there's nothing there," commented Virgil.

"I'll have one of you fellas kneeling down and pointing to something at your feet." Jack demonstrated. "I'll shoot the angle so that the readers will not see the ground."

"And I'll frighten the bejezzus out of them with my description of the little, helpless girl just inches away from that giant viper." Harry paused, writing the tag lines in his mind. *"The fearful buzzing of the viper's rattling tail drowned out the hammering of the child's heart."*

Jack Chase was long ago vaccinated against the vivid purple of Harry's prose. The photographer shook his head and snickered. "After that, there won't be a garter snake left alive anywhere in New York State."

Jack bent down to position Shorty for their contrived picture. He whispered, "Pure bullshit, but old man Pulitzer will love it."

As Jack stood and moved to the back of his tripod, Harry's eyes widened at his newest brainstorm. "Virgil, can you find us a snake?"

"No Harry, we don't have time for me to rustle up one now." He paused and concentrated on holding back a grin.

"I tell you what, while Jack gets the picture, why don't you head off into the brush over there and look for one." With three seconds of pondering the idea concluded, Harry Hamlet decided to forgo the snake. When Jack's pictures were taken, the four began to remount.

Jack and Shorty were already in the saddle. Virgil waited until Harry got one foot into a stirrup. He simultaneously delivered a poke to the writer's side and a made a loud faux buzz to his ear. Knowing what was coming, Shorty had moved his mount next to Harry's horse and was stroking the mare's mane. Harry screamed as he tried to turn and run, both at the same time. His foot didn't clear the stirrup and down he went.

Virgil reached down a hand and helped Harry up. "He was a biggun'. Did you hear how loud he was? His two red eyes were…glowing."

Harry was smart enough to smile as he dusted himself off. The joke was one of his own making.

The four rode on. In another hour they arrived at McGinty's cold camp on the banks of Tabor Creek. As before, all the details were described to Harry. Virgil showed where the stolen horse was tied. He described how the animal's clustered footprints and the smell of its urine revealed where it had been hidden while McGinty snuck into town. Again Harry's prepared questions were answered. Jack took more pictures for the editor to review.

The men continued on down the creek as McGinty had done until they reached the Mary's River. As they stood at

McGinty's entry point, Virgil made sure to describe what the river waters were like back in April. The hard, cold, and fast water of the spring run-off was opposite to how the Mary's looked in mid-August. The snow was melted on all but the highest of the Humboldt Mountain peaks. The river at their feet, now shallow, slow moving and warm from the Nevada sun, was not the same as the waters that had taken McGinty's life.

Next Virgil described how the posse had split into separate search parties for each side of the river. Verrall Black's plan, while thorough and well executed, failed to locate the bandit. Finding the riderless stolen horse on the far side was a clue. When the body appeared the next day its condition—torn clothes and ripped flesh—suggested a scenario.

"Some of the boys thought that a mountain lion grabbed him. Then he went in the river by accident and bled to death in the water." Virgil paused, waiting for questions; none came.

"Sam Winnemucca was looking at the body. Sam's a professional hunter, so he's seen deer carcasses from lion kills. Well then, Sam sees these little bruises, just dots, mind you. Anyway, he does a little knife work and what do you know, under each bruise was a big pine splinter...Imagine that!"

Harry paused from his note taking. "And what did that tell you about how Bill McGinty died?"

"You know everything that made it into the story in the Elko paper. We figured it this way. Here are the pieces. We find where he tried to cross. The river was at its peak. His horse is across the river and unhurt. There were no boot tracks across the river and then we find his body in the river. His left side is all busted up."

"Busted how?"

"Leg, arm and hip were all broke. Then those big gashes in his chest and finally the splinters embedded in his chest. All those things taken together made us pretty sure that a big 'widow maker' log hit him while he was crossing the river. Maybe it knocks him out, who knows, but he's bleeding bad and drowns. His body gets stuck somewhere until it washes up by our camp the next day."

Harry added to his notes and conferred with Jack for the best set of pictures to accompany the story. Then Harry asked his questions about what brought people from all over the West to Deeth. Where was the vanished $7000?

Virgil framed the last question of the day. "It's getting late. If you want to try your hand at finding the payroll or see anything else out here, we must camp for the night. If not, we can make it back to town tonight. It's up to you."

"Tomorrow is our last day with you fellas, correct?"

"Nyup," replied Shorty and Virgil continued. "Yeah, we're due back to the cattle company, day after tomorrow. The time is yours to do what you like. You can stay here until noon tomorrow and still have enough time for us to get back and we'll introduce you to Samuel. If he talks is up to him."

Harry huddled with Jack before answering. With all the information about the robbery and McGinty's later crime in his possession, Harry Hamlet only needed to interview Verrall Black and Samuel Winnemucca, and if permitted, speak to Sam's daughter. "Let's camp. We can scout the river bank for the money. Tomorrow morning on our way, point out likely spots where McGinty might have hidden or even buried the cash."

Over coffee around their campfire on the banks of the Mary's, the lost loot was discussed. "Here's how Shorty and I see it. We don't think that McGinty would have crossed the river with the money hidden on this side."

"Why?" asked Jack.

"Well if he came back for the money, he risked being recognized. We think he wanted to get gone and stay gone."

"So he kept the money with him and it went into the river when he did." Harry kicked the unburned end of a branch further into the camp fire, raising a cloud of sparks as he spoke.

"So where is it now?"

"I believe it's still in the river. If I were hunting the money I'd be watching both river banks to see if she gives up the money like she gave up McGinty's body.

Harry turned his eyes towards Shorty. "Shorty, you agree?"

"Nyup" was his reply and the four new friends decided to turn in for the night.

* * *

Their last morning on the trail was spent walking the Mary's river banks starting back upstream where McGinty had tried to ford the spring torrent. The river was now low enough to allow a man to wade, but Jack and Shorty took their horses across, anyway. The piles of debris and pools between protruding rocks were all checked for the missing money bag. What the river hid one day might be waiting in plain sight the next. Four hours of searching revealed nothing, and the enterprise was abandoned at noon.

The actual race was not between the river and the seekers, but between paper and water. The Mary's had given up the cash bag, as it had given up McGinty's body. It drifted down the Mary's and into the Humboldt River. By the time the bag stopped outside Carlin, Nevada, south of Elko, the money was one sodden mass hiding in a slimy leather skin. There it lay along the river bank, the leather drying and cracking. The money, tight inside, now solidified into one indistinguishable lump which gradually subsided into the river bottom silt.

* * *

Back in Deeth, the four parted with a plan to meet for dinner. Harry and Jack were quick to embrace the joys of a bath and clean clothes. Virgil and Shorty dealt with the company horses and gear. Then they embraced the joys of beer. After Virgil cleared the dust from his throat with a medicinal ale, he walked to the Paiute village.

Respectful of Paiute ways, Virgil called out, "Hello, Samuel," from outside the wickiup. The first head to emerge from the dim light of the hut was Sam's. He invited his guest to take a seat on one of the log rounds that surrounded their firepit. Virgil recapped the days with the newspaper men.

"The reporter fella, Harry Hamlet would like to talk to you. Would you be willing to give him a few minutes tomorrow morning?" Sam agreed. Only a messenger, Virgil was reluctant to relay Hamlet's other requests. Could Hamlet speak to Galli, under parental supervision?

The answer was "No."

Would Samuel allow the photographer to take a picture of the family and of the outside of their home?

The Paiute hunter kept his eyes on the ashes in the fire pit but said nothing. Virgil got up to leave, but stopped to add a sweetener.

"Why don't you think about the pictures and tell him tomorrow. I'll make sure that there's money in it for your family. Think about it." The tall cowboy offered his hand to the silent Sam. They shook hands and went back to their business.

* * *

As the four men shared their last night together, Virgil gave Harry directions for tomorrow's meeting with Samuel Winnemucca. Then Virgil explained how the request to take photographs was received and that Harry would get an answer direct from the Paiute tomorrow.

"Make a very respectful 'thank you' offer to Samuel. These are proud folks. Jack should be nearby, but not with you when you first meet him."

"Good idea, and thanks for asking on my behalf."

Over their last drink of the evening, Harry answered Shorty's question about their plans.

"The Winnemuccas tomorrow morning, and then we'll interview Verrall Black. We're on the last train heading west in the afternoon. Mr. Pulitzer pulled some political strings with your Governor and we're on our way to interview Ben Kuhl and Ed Beck at the prison outside Carson City. After that, it's back East."

* * *

Harry Hamlet got his interview with Samuel. Jack Chase got to photograph the Winnemucca family standing together outside their wickiup. The family received a twenty-dollar thank you from Pulitzer's *New York World* newspaper.

Later, they also immortalized Verrall Black in both print and picture.

The two imprisoned robbers, with no secrets to bargain, accepted cigarettes for cooperating with interviews and picture. In their striped prison garb, with numbers stenciled across their chests, the two were photographed by the prison's front gate, flanked by shotgun-toting guards.

Harry Hamlet took home four full books of notes, some already having been incorporated into daily reports. Jack Chase had snapped over two hundred photographs. They left behind the polio virus in everyone with whom they'd come in contact.

Hamlet's articles and Chase's pictures ran on Page One for a solid ten days. The virus was the unwanted gift that kept on giving for a long time.

9. The Plague, September 1916

Melba Black had just turned fourteen years. Having never missed a meal or gone without new clothes or shelter, her life was good.

"Mother, my neck's stiff. It's been this way since I woke up this morning and my head aches."

Since Melba's father owned the town store, the family had on hand a supply of patent medicines. Libby Black didn't discount her daughter's discomforts. She put them down as part of the September heat and the searing wind that had persisted for several days. When Melba's discomforts did not resolve themselves, Libby Black spoke to her husband.

"Verrall, I'm taking Melba over to Doc Miller. She's not getting any better."

Her husband nodded in agreement as he left the house for his store.

Doctor Maynard Miller had studied medicine at the Harvard Medical School. Deeply religious, his powerful beliefs about slavery motivated him to enlist in the Union Army in 1864. He remained in service after the Civil War and was reposted out West. The Indian Wars still required his practiced skills in treating gunshot and stab wounds. He ended his Army career as company surgeon at Ft. Huachuca, Arizona.

Miller had gained an appreciation for the beauty of the high desert and rugged mountains. He opened his retirement practice at Deeth in 1916. Widowed and in his 76th year, Doc Miller had lost none of his curiosity or medical skills. He regularly read the latest in medical literature arriving from back East. The quiet of a high desert town suited him just fine.

Libby tapped on the bedroom door. "Melba, get up, honey. Let's go over to Dr. Miller and see what he thinks is wrong with you."

"Yes, Momma." Then came her panicked cry. "Momma, my legs feel funny and I can't stand up. I'm scared, Momma."

"Come quick, Momma." Libby rushed into the bedroom. Melba's thirteen-year-old sister was standing in her nightgown at Melba's side, a hand on each of the other girl's shoulders. "Momma, if I let go of her she tips over."

Libby heard the alarm in the child's voice. Concealing her own growing concern, she replaced Doris at the bedside, her hands now holding Melba's shoulders. Her daughter's back had stiffened into a stooped curve from hips to shoulders.

Libby's immediate task was to comfort her child. She sat down on Melba's bed, still clutching her shoulders. "Doris, get dressed quick. Run over to Dr. Miller's office and tell the doctor we need him to come over here as quick as he can. Say 'please' when you ask. Then I want you to go to your Dad's store and tell him he needs to come home. Can you do that for me, please?" and Libby struggled to hold back tears.

Doris was out the door in record time with her nightgown traded for a dress and boots on bare feet. Underwear and socks could wait. Across three dusty blocks, she knocked as loudly as she dared on the doctor's office door.

"Come in," the doctor called as he put down the morning mail he'd been reviewing. "Good morning, Doris."

The youthful messenger stood in the open doorway and delivered her message, which ended with a "please." Her tone and her panting said all the doctor needed to rouse him from his swivel chair. Doc Miller picked up his medical bag and was out the door. His 76-year-old's pace far behind the thirteen-year-old messenger's, he took the child's hand. "Walk with me and tell me about your sister."

Doris escorted Doc Miller up the porch steps, where she opened the front door. "Melba is upstairs in our room. You can go on up. I'm supposed to go tell my Dad." The old man and the teen were still holding hands.

"Honey, how about you wait until I look at your sister?"

"But Momma said…"

Her worried voice was silenced by a calming gesture from the doctor. "I know. I'll tell your mother it was my idea, so you won't be in any trouble." He waited as Doris bit her lower lip. "Now I don't need another worried parent around my patient. Wouldn't it be better for us to bring your Dad when we have something to tell him?"

Her eyes darting around the walls and ceiling, Doris agreed.

"All right then, take me to your sister."

Up the stairs they went. At the bedroom door, Doc Miller read Libby Black's face; panicked at her daughter's condition and angry that Doris had not gone to fetch Verrall Black.

Miller spoke first. "Mrs. Black, I told Doris to wait on getting her Dad until I could tell him something, other than to wait out of my way."

The rigid lines in Libby Black's face let go of their anger, sagging into a mask of concern.

"If you would please let me take your place, while you move down to the foot of the bed," he said in a calm, patient voice. With 55 years of practiced bedside manner, he smiled and sat at Melba's side.

He helped Melba lie back as he asked her questions about her symptoms. After each answer, Miller glanced to the mother for confirmation or correction. What he saw was not new to him: symptoms uncommon here but not unknown. From the newspapers and medical journals which he read daily, the doctor knew about the East Coast polio epidemic.

Taking great care to ease any concerns about modesty, he asked if he could raise her gown to mid-thigh. He palpated her legs, feeling the rigidity of their flesh through his fingertips. When Melba's legs had told their story, he respectfully pulled down the hem of her gown.

"I'm going to run my fingers over your gown, along your spine and shoulders. Tell me if anything hurts?" When his examination was completed, it strengthened his working diagnosis. The disease had arrived.

"Mrs. Black, you can send Doris to fetch her Father now. Melba, I'm going to be downstairs in the parlor and visit with your folks. I promise to come back to see you before I go. Are you all right with that, young lady?"

"Yes," came her whispered answer, and the two adults left the room.

* * *

"Verrall."

"Maynard." Melba's Father sat stiff backed at the family's dining table. His tension traveled down his arm and into his wife's hand, which he gripped. Doris stayed upstairs with her sister.

"I'll tell you what I know, don't know and suspect. That's the best I can do, and none of its good."

The dour Scotsman nodded his understanding.

"I believe Melba has come down with what we call polio. There's a longer name, but it doesn't sound any better. Doctors don't know what causes polio or how to cure it. I'm sorry." Dr. Miller let those two brutal facts register; then he continued.

"I suspect that she is in the worst part of the disease, the first seven days. After that time, the virus will have settled into those muscles in Melba's body where it intends to stay. We don't yet know where those muscles will be." And he stopped. Libby was sobbing, and the doctor had lost Verrall Black in his own thoughts.

"We need to take the child to the hospital in Elko. She's going to need full time care until this acute stage passes. After that, we'll figure out what to do. I'm sorry."

Her parents took Melba Black to the Elko County Hospital. Libby Black remained almost constantly at her side. Verrall arranged with the Commercial Hotel for a room to always be available. Her mother's pain somehow matched Melba's agony as the child screamed, enduring therapy sessions intended to release her spine from the strangle hold of her infected muscles. Finally the invader settled in Melba's legs, rendering them unable to hold up even her diminished weight.

Dr. Maynard Miller found that Melba Black was to be the first of many polio victims in his once-quiet little town.

* * *

The doctor was busy enough treating Vivian McDowell, a housekeeper and server at Mrs. Nicely's boarding house where Harry and Jack had stayed. After Vivian, fresh cases in the white community began appearing almost daily, vectored through the mercantile, Cannon's saloon or the cattle company.

Dr. Miller sent Vivian McDowell to the Elko County Hospital. When she returned, the virus had settled in her right arm and leg, rendering both useless. The capricious killer settled wherever it pleased, if its host survived the first seven days.

On the same September morning, Pamahas Winnemucca, and seven-year-old Tony Besa-Yoona', the little fry bread seller, were both struck down by polio. Pamahas had delivered more than deerskin gloves to the Black's mercantile. She unknowingly delivered the polio virus, if it wasn't already there.

The Deeth Paiute band was unaware of this new white man's disease. The Northern Paiutes didn't turn to white doctors. They believed curing the body while ignoring the soul left only a husk and not a whole person.

Pamahas wasn't feeling well. Her headache and a fever persisted. Even lying still brought no relief from her back pains. She guessed venison, left too long or dried too little,

104

to be the cause of her distress. As the day rolled into evening, her discomfort increased. Sage bloom tea hadn't helped. When she was unable to rise from her bed on the second morning, Samuel knew he needed help.

This small group did not have its own shaman, so Samuel sought the help of the tribal healers, the shamans of the Wells and Elko Paiute bands. His act of love by seeking help unintentionally linked the Deeth outbreak to other Northern Nevada bands. And so the virus spread.

Polio's attack on Pamahas Winnemucca settled in her chest muscles and not her legs. The efforts of two shamans gave her no comfort as she struggled to draw breath. Watching helplessly from her side, Samuel suffered along with each of her labored breaths. He did what he could. He learned to fear the wet, gurgling, strangling sound of saliva drowning her struggling lungs. He'd lift her torso with one brawny arm, forcing her head down and slapping her back, like he'd done years before burping their daughter. Laying her back down, he forced her chin down as mucus and saliva drained from her nostrils. Such simple acts of love were all that he had to ease her suffering.

Samuel Winnemucca, finally despairing of the shamans power, carried his wife in his arms to the doctor. When Maynard Miller examined the new patient, his diagnosis was not in doubt: polio. All of his training and experience didn't provide him any means to help Pamahas, so instead he ministered to Samuel. The two men turned Pamahas onto her side, making it easier to clear her nose and throat. Only being able to offer momentary relief was cold comfort for a healer whose career was fighting death as a mortal enemy. The two men shared the vigil at her side.

"If she survives the week, I'll send her to a hospital in Salt Lake City. They have specialized equipment that can help her breathe. We just have to wait. I'm so sorry, my friend."

Samuel made eye contact with the doctor then silently returned his gaze to his wife's tortured face.

Dr. Miller excused himself and left Samuel at his wife's side. The old doctor donned his coat and hat, even in the September heat, for that was his most professional image. He knew the Paiute village must be checked for other cases. At the cluster of wickiups, Dr. Miller encountered an unanticipated problem: distrust between the white and Indian communities.

Among the eight families in this Paiute band, all but one had some interaction with the white citizenry. They worked as domestics, laborers, or cowboys. Interacting with their white neighbors was common; the acceptance of white medicine or religion were not. Now polio was loose. Isolated cases became an epidemic innocently spread by the smallest, invisible saliva droplets that traveled in so many sneezes and coughs. Families now spread the virus through the school, saloons and Post Office.

News traveled fast in the tiny village. The situation in the Winnemucca family was common knowledge, as was the two shamans' inability to heal Pamahas. That Dr. Miller had tried to help Pamahas was the reassurance the Besa-Yoona' family needed to allow daughter Tony to be seen.

The child lay on her deerskin bed, her eyes glassy, beads of perspiration on her forehead. "May I touch her?" asked Dr. Miller.

The mother gave permission with a silent nod.

Miller knelt by the little girl. Her brow was hot to his touch. "Where does she have pain?" Her mother gestured to her own neck and upper arm.

The diagnosis was obvious. The virus had struck again. Miller needed to know, would the Elko hospital treat an Indian patient? Did her path to treatment run through the Bureau of Indian Affairs? God, he hoped not. Dr. Miller's experience inside Indian country gave him no confidence in the government's willingness to provide even mandated services to Native Americans. He'd not make any promises until he knew how they would be received.

"Keep her cool with a wet cloth on her forehead. Come tell me if the child gets worse or has trouble breathing. This may pass by the end of the week. We have to wait and see. May I come back tomorrow and look in on…?" and he stopped, unsure of the child's name.

The mother provided the prompt, "Tony. Yes, come tomorrow."

As he walked away, Maynard Miller thought back to Pamahas and Samuel at her side. He'd let them both stay in his office. It was as good a place for her to die as anywhere else.

* * *

Pamahas Winnemucca escaped her suffering two nights later. Samuel had not left her side. Dr. Miller was a helpless observer. He vanished when Samuel had to deal with her bodily functions. She became unable to swallow when the paralysis reached her throat. When she passed, Miller knew Pamahas had fought as long and hard as she could. She died of exhaustion from fighting her own frozen muscles in order to breathe.

Tony's mother, Pahninee worked as a dishwasher in the kitchen at the Cannon saloon and dance hall where she was called 'Polly.' The saloon's new owner, Phineas Franklin, had promoted his reliable kitchen worker to server. Franklin had not upped Polly's pay, and she still washed dishes. But her table service provided opportunities for tips from appreciative diners such as Harry Hamlet. And so the polio virus gained another vector.

* * *

The two shamans took quiet satisfaction in hearing that Pamahas had died in the white doctor's office. If their medicine had failed, so too had the white man's. So were the

107

white ways any better, stronger? They agreed; the Indian way was better. They failed only because their personal medicine had not been powerful enough. With all the bands now suffering from polio's invasion, the shamans knew they needed the power of the Ghost Dance to heal their people.

Only the strength of all the Paiutes and their collective 1000 feet dancing and praying together would vanquish the invisible killer in their midst. Every band: Tuscarora, Wells, Winnemucca, Elko, Battle Mountain, and Paradise Valley had to come together. The two shamans sent word to the most distant of their blood. The added power of the Snake Indians and the Klamath-Paiutes from Oregon was also needed. And they came.

Indian Hill at Deeth was to be the place for the great Ghost Dance. Each band's shaman told his people, "Bring your sick to be healed." Five hundred Indians came to Deeth, two weeks after the shamans' call. They came in cars, on the backs of trucks, by horse and even some on foot. Their clothes were a visible sign of an Indian diaspora. Blanket coats of many colors and skin garments were equal in number to bought or made cloth attire.

Wilson Finch donated two steers per day for the 500 souls who'd come to town. Before the dancing began, Paiute hunters harvested the local deer. Once the women had erected a shelter, they foraged for tender cattail shoots. Bands that didn't bring poles for wickiup frames used sage brush or juniper branches to cover hollowed-out below-ground shelters, with blankets draped as covers over their sage roof. Permanence was never intended. Everyone understood that their energy was being saved for the dancing. The shamans promised that if they danced hard enough, their people could escape from the white man's plague.

10. The Fear, October 1916

Dr. Miller made daily rounds through the camp. With Samuel Winnemucca at his side, the two stopped at every shelter. Most ignored the doctor, and he was unwelcome in many of the shelters. He often saw their sick lying inside, being tended by family members. Some victims needed help to breathe, like Pamahas.

Death, fear and suspicion ratcheted up together as polio tightened its grip on the town and the Paiute bands. Because the methods of transmission were still unknown or misunderstood, the townspeople tried anything and everything. Prayer was no more effective than wearing garlic around one's neck, flowers in your pocket or burning sulfur wicks in the house. When the infection rate topped 20%, everyone knew one of the hundred victims in town. Polio was right next door, if not already in your house.

* * *

In every house in Deeth, fear-laden words were being spoken.

"Danny, don't go in the river. It will make you sick."

"Yes, Mama."

"Mabel, honey, I don't want you anywhere near that dirty Indian village. Do you understand?"

"Yes, Ma."

"Tommy, stay away from those Hartford boys. They live too close to the village."

Stay away from the Italians. They are low-class and dirty. Stay away from the poor. They're dirty too. And so it went.

Fear of the invisible turned neighbor against neighbor. The local Paiutes were especially hard hit. Those that worked for white employers lost their jobs, because this was an "Indian disease." Everybody believed it.

109

The town watched as the Paiute encampment grew until its crescent shape almost enclosed the base of Indian Hill. The river became their water source upstream and their latrine, downstream. Mumblings of "those dirty Indians" or worse became common among the wives and mothers in Deeth. When fear starts in the home, its transfer into the saloons comes pre-approved.

"Austin, those filthy Indians are bringing their disease to town. What are we going to do? They brought their sick. They shit in the river. My God, we're going to come down with the Indian virus." The fearful voices in the homes spread to husbands and from husbands to the bars and the wider community. Unreasoning fear, stoked by ignorance, spilled forth on their whisky breath.

"They're gonna be dancing for five days and another two days clearin' out. Who among you already has the sickness in your own folks?" Austin Cannon leaned back, took a hard pull on his whisky and waited.

The question circulated around the other five at the barroom table. The others talked among themselves. The implication of Austin's question hung in the smoke-filled air, unanswered.

"Ask your wives if they expect you to do something." Pausing to give each face a tough, questioning look, Austin continued. "Well, are you?" and he slammed his glass down on the table top, sloshing the amber contents on the table and floor. They sat, trading glances, and Sarge appeared at the table side.

"This reminds me of back in '90 at Wounded Knee." Twelve eyes locked on his stubble-covered face. Cannon poured more whiskey into his own glass and slid it over in front of Sarge Daniels. No one spoke.

"Some of those red devils had guns. When a couple of troopers started to collect their guns, a fight broke out. Then a gun went off and my friend Jackie Jameson dropped, shot dead. Then our company did what we should have done to begin with." Sarge banged the table top with the broom stick held in his hand and drained the glass of whiskey. Now bent and gray, the onetime horse soldier put down the empty glass, lifted his broom from the table and returned to sweeping.

* * *

On the third day, with the bands assembled, the Ghost Dance began. Seven shamans took turns leading the dance from the center of the giant circle. Three hundred dancers were all that could dance at one time on the sacred top of Indian Hill. Men, women, and children all danced. Clockwise around, they danced to the beat of the ten drummers and ten singers. Two steps forward, side shuffle out and back, dancing until they dropped. When dancers fell in the line, other Paiutes helped them up and out, only to be replaced in the never-stopping circle.

The sound of the dance was now a background to every conversation in town. Near Indian Hill, the stomp of 600 feet coupled with their drum beat caused folks to check the train tracks for the locomotive they could hear, but not yet see.

Phineas Franklin, owner of a saloon and dance hall, commanded attention. He was wealthy, ergo he must be smart. Men enjoying a free drink were quick to conclude as much. His physical presence was imposing; Phin was six foot ten inches tall. He had been the first to fire his Paiute employees. His staff was reduced to Ed the bartender, Mary the cook, and Sarge the sweeper. Former cavalry Sergeant Dan Daniels and his remembrances of Wounded Knee became more prominent.

"Sarge, come have a drink and tell me more about 1890 and the Sioux."

"Well boss, our outfit, the Old 7th Cavalry, didn't enjoy seeing Indians with guns. You know why." Sarge was telling rather than asking. Everybody in the West knew about General G.A. Custer and "Little Bighorn."

"All we wanted was to take their guns away. But those red devils resisted and then," stopping to swig whisky. "What the hell else could we do?" The old soldier stared into his glass for an answer.

"We shot every one of those bastards we could. Bucks, squaws, kids; we shot 'em all. Then we took their guns."

Phineas refilled his sweeper's glass, his mind now made up. He held court at a barroom table. The more he poured, the more sense he made to the some of the twelve men around him. Everyone in the saloon had the polio in their home or with someone they knew. His speech sounded reasonable.

"Every Paiute in Nevada is in our town. Some of them brought guns. It's bad enough that they brought their disease," and he topped off twelve shot glasses. "They have no need for guns here in our town. None whatsoever." Silent while he made eye contact with each man, Franklin then continued.

"I, for one, would feel a hell of a lot better if we collected those guns for safe keeping. That's all, and we'll return them when they leave." Again he checked each man's face as he sank the hook. "Do you see any harm in that?" Some of the twelve nodded in agreement while others cut their eyes down to their drinks or looked sideways to the next man. Four of the group drank their shot and quietly left.

"No thanks, Phin. You're courtin' trouble there. We will not get involved."

Deputies Graves and McCabe were keeping a finger on the pulse of their town. "Can we stop this?" McCabe had asked his partner when Franklin's full scheme was revealed.

"I don't think so, but we sure as hell can't be involved." There was no doubt in Jim Graves's mind. This was an all-around bad idea. The two deputies rose and two more men joined them. Phin Franklin watched as they turned their backs and left his saloon.

"Some men don't have the stomach to step up and do what's right. It's a damn shame." Only brothers Arthur and Tom Griswold, Ike Edison, and Austin Cannon remained. Cannon's daughter Marjorie had died of the virus. The long silence endured until their table mates had departed. All the eyes of the remaining men now focused on Phin Franklin.

"There are three more days of dancing and two days after that while they break camp. If we're going to do this thing, best we do it now. Go home, get a gun and meet back here. Wear a coat to cover your gun. We want to be inconspicuous."

The four left.

Franklin got five lanterns from his store room. The dark gave the men cover to move around the encampment, but they would need light to see inside the Indian dwellings. Then he put on his coat and tucked a .32 caliber Colt pistol into his belt.

His accomplices returned and each was now armed.

'Phin, how are we going to do this?" asked Austin Cannon.

"We walk into the Indian village and begin checking wickiups, lean-tos and dugouts for guns. Be polite but firm. Ask if there are any guns there. If they show you one or if you see one," with heavy emphasis on his next two words, "TAKE IT. Tell them we'll return the guns when they leave town. Simple."

"I may need some help here," said Tom, the younger of the Griswold brothers. The other four plotters turned to him, unsure of what he meant. "Hey look, I've got a lantern in one hand. I need my other hand free to go for my gun. If I see a rifle standing in the corner, what do I do, tuck it under my arm and carry it into the next place?"

"Okay, okay, I'll bring a big cloth sack to carry any guns we find." Franklin didn't want anyone's resolve to fade. "You fellas will search and I'll stay outside with the bag and keep a lookout."

I like that even better, because I'm out of harm's way. "Ready?"

The moon loomed large over the town as the five walked toward Indian Hill. Deputy Jim Graves watched them pass as he sat alone in the dark, hidden in the shadow of the Sheriff's office porch. A red glowing tip from his cheroot was the only sign of his presence. The five were all men he'd sat with at Phin Franklin's table. Since they appeared unarmed, he ignored their passing.

The night air vibrated from the 300 pairs of feet and ten drums struck all together in a never-ending thump. Franklin and his accomplices could see clearly under the bright Harvest Moon. They kept their voices low. One hundred and fifty separate shelters tailed off in a crescent surrounding the base of Indian Hill. The Griswold brothers would begin the search on the left horn of the crescent. Ike Edison and Austin Cannon would enter from the right.

"All right now, check every shelter. Don't miss any. I'll be right behind you, out here. If you find a gun, one of you bring it back to me. I'll keep a lookout," assured Franklin. *And stay the heck away from any trouble.* The pounding of feet and drums obscured any sounds from the shelters. In the moonlight, they saw only a few solitary figures coming or going from the river.

Up ahead Tom Griswold saw two Paiute men helping an exhausted dancer down the slope of the hill to his shelter. A Paiute woman in an ornately beaded deer skin dress walked past the descending three and up to take a place in the dance.

Unnoticed, the brothers approached the first Paiute shelter: hollowed out from the sandy earth, a domed cover of sage brush branches topped with blankets. The dark interior allowed entry down a dug-out ramp. Art Griswold

115

took the lead. Trying to bend over while on his feet proved unworkable, and the big man got down on his knees to enter. He held his lantern out in front and poked his head inside the dug-out. Two sleeping children looked back towards the light and then closed their eyes. Art surveyed the interior, looking for guns. Unwilling to roust sleeping children, he backed out. He silently shook his head, and the brothers moved on.

Austin Cannon and Ike Edison had unknowingly started with the Deeth Paiutes' permanent wickiups. Their willow bough frames with reed coverings used a blanket as a door covering. Lantern in hand, the two had agreed to take turns entering, while the other posted up outside the doorway. Ike entered first and knowing some small amount of Indian customs, he discretely patted the blanket cover door and call out to any occupant. "Public safety, I'm going to come in," and then he pulled back the blanket with his free hand and thrust the lantern inside.

The lantern light shone on a grandmother sitting on the floor, soothing a child whose head she cradled in her lap. Neither one spoke. The old mother's eyes registered surprise as Ike scanned the interior walls for guns. The child's breathing fixed his attention. *Plague, oh shit!* He backed out.

"Only an old woman and a kid, but no guns that I could see. Let's go." And the pair moved on to the next wickiup. Three times more they found empty lodgings, sleeping children, the elderly, or the sick.

The fifth wickiup was the Winnemuccas'. Important as the Ghost Dance was to the health of the Paiute nation, feeding his brothers and sisters was even more important, so Samuel was out hunting the mule deer that populated the mountain foothills. Carrying a deer carcass was slow going. It was well after dark before he made it back.

Austin Cannon didn't share his partner's sense of propriety for announcing himself before entering. He passed through the blanket door cover. In the light of a small fire he faced an unclad, thirteen-year-old Galli. With her nakedness on full display, the uplift of her breasts and her cascading black hair bracketed a look of surprise. She made no move to cover herself before the intruder and challenged him, "What do you want?"

Cannon saw what he'd come for against the wickiup's back wall. Behind where Galli stood was a double-barrel shotgun. He stepped inside and circled toward Galli around the small fire. Galli half-turned to grab a knife from its resting place on the fire ring. When she did, Cannon drew his pistol and shot her in the lower back. Stunned by the impact, she turned to face the intruder and his second shot pierced her breast. Galli fell onto her back, motionless.

With his ears ringing from the shots, Cannon watched the scarlet flow from her wounds. Death took Galli Winnemucca quickly. As blood pooled on the deerskin-covered floor beneath her hips, Cannon ignored the shotgun and fled. "Let's get out of here. I killed her."

The boom of shots roused every adult in the camp. Edison and Cannon moved back the way they'd come toward Phin Franklin, both men with their guns drawn. Behind them voices cried out in the Paiute tongue. Behind his two approaching men, Phin Franklin saw more men, some dressed, others in only breech-cloths, pouring out of their shelters and forming groups.

Samuel Winnemucca carried a black-tail doe carcass over his big shoulders. He steadied his load with one hand, his rifle clutched in the other. The great camp was in sight when the shots rang out. He doubled his pace as he approached.

Jimmy Hokwaits from the Wells Paiute band stopped him as he approached.

"The white man shot Galilhai."

Samuel dropped the deer from his shoulders, sprinted towards his wickiup and entered.

Kneeling at her side, he touched his child's face, still warm but slack in death. He gently closed her eyes with his fingertips. With blood pooling beneath her hips and the only visible wound to her breast, he concluded RAPE. Tears filled the hunter's eyes as he rose to his feet. Standing over his daughter's naked, dead body, his thoughts turned dark. Nothing taken—naked—surprised by a white intruder—why?

Jimmy Hokwaits waited outside as Samuel emerged. Jimmy's wife and oldest daughter stood behind him, their heads bent low. The women silently moved behind Samuel and into the death house. They would clean and cover Galli's body, as had been Paiute woman's work forever.

Samuel turned and gripped Jimmy's forearm, unaware of the crushing force his anger and sorrow imparted. "Which white man did this?"

Hokwaits didn't know Deeth citizens by name, so he repeated the description of the two whites seen hurrying away from the murder scene. Samuel acknowledged his understanding with a small nod. He knew Jimmy was his band's hunter.

"Get your rifle and protect the people. Tell the other hunters to protect our people from the white killers. I'm going to avenge my daughter," he said in Paiute. As Jimmy turned, the iron grip stopped him for one more question. "Which way?"

Jimmy pointed.

Word spread quickly around the camp and to the shamans. Not daring to stop the sacred healing power of the ritual, the dance was not immediately interrupted. But in every visitor's shelter, guns came out and armed men filled the camp. Inside their shelters, Paiute women clutched knives or clubs, ready to resist white invaders.

Francis Huascari, a hunter from the Tuscarora band, was the first to spot the Griswolds. When the two shots rang out the brothers had stopped their searching and headed back to find Phin Franklin. In the brief minutes after the killing, all Francis heard was white men had raped and killed a Paiute girl. His first shot struck Tom Griswold in the calf.

Art pulled his brother to cover behind the nearest sagebrush dome. Both men drew their guns. Shots rang out from both sides as more Indian guns spit smoke and fire into the night.

Phin Franklin desperately searched for cover at the sound of the first shots. Off to his right side Edison and Cannon were running his way. Franklin had no stomach for the chaos and death his plan had spawned. He broke from cover and ran.

Samuel Winnemucca watched the tall man run back towards town. He instantly recognized Phineas Franklin, whom he knew by sight.

The first shots propelled Jim Graves out of his contented smoke and back inside his office. Bill McCabe was already up and tugging on his boots. "Shots at the village. Grab a rifle and let's go." A short two blocks away, the same two shots interrupted the quiet evening in the Black's home.

"Libby, you and the girls stay inside. I'm going over to the sheriff's to see what's going on." As Verrall Black tied his shoes and put on a shirt over suspenders, Deputies Graves and McCabe, now armed, were moving toward the Paiute encampment.

Ike Edison and Austin Cannon watched Franklin run away. They, too, looked for cover, but too late, as Samuel's first shot took Edison in the small of the back and he fell down, unable to rise. Austin Cannon, Galli's killer, was trying to drag his friend out of the open. Samuel's second shot exploded his head. Ike Edison lay awake with his mind clear as a shadow fell across his face and blocked the moon. Samuel Winnemucca chambered another round, pointed the rifle muzzle to Ike's forehead. The two men's eyes met and Samuel pulled the trigger.

In the same moment that the deputies arrived, Verrall Black discovered their office open and empty. The continuing nearby gunfire sounded muffled to the partially deaf leader of the "Citizens Civil Order Committee." His better judgment prevailed; knowing that acting too soon was as bad as acting too late, he started walking to the school house. When the bell sounded, every good man in town would answer the call. Black would form his group, determine what was needed and then lead from the front.

The Griswolds were pinned down by Francis Huascari and three other guns firing from the dark. Tom and Art fired at any shadow or moving form. Two Paiutes died, and another two were wounded before they'd emptied their guns. Four unseen Paiute shooters moved closer, intent on finishing the two white intruders.

Samuel arrived, coming up behind the brothers' position. He saw the Griswold brother's fall to the bullets of the other shooters. *They can't hang me any higher for killing four whites than for killing two.*

Hearing the approach of the deputies, he turned, showing himself before slipping off into the shadows. Graves and McCabe, unsure of how many shooters, crouched low over the two white bodies. They heard Samuel's voice from the dark.

"I killed the four white men who raped and killed my daughter." And then the voice was gone.

The two deputies stood, guns at their sides, and backed out of the camp. Their immediate plan was to escape alive and call Elko for reinforcement. Who had died was unknown, but to stay in the camp now meant to die from an unseen gun somewhere out in the dark, They would return tomorrow with other deputies.

* * *

Verrall Black and fifteen men from the Citizens Committee stood silently outside the sheriff's station when Jim Graves and Bill McCabe reappeared from the Paiute village. Were they needed, and for what purpose? Verrall stepped forward. That both deputies were carrying rifles told him a great deal before they spoke the first word.

"I heard the shots. I guess we all did. What happened? How can we help?"

Jim Graves carried his rifle in the crook of his arm. Bill McCabe set the butt of his rifle down and held the barrel, the muzzle pointed straight up. Graves scanned the faces of the men before he spoke. "Samuel Winnemucca shot four men, killed 'em all."

"Who died?" Black voiced the question that was on fifteen minds.

"Ike Edison, Austin Cannon and the Griswold brothers." Graves left unsaid that those four and Phin Franklin had gone together to the village. What happened to Franklin was an immediate concern, but not something for the committee.

"Why did he kill 'em? Did he say?"

"Samuel confessed that he killed all four of them. He said that they had raped and killed his daughter." Looks and mumbled words passed between the committee members. Samuel Winnemucca and his family were well known to Verrall Black, and not unknown to most of the others.

"Is it true? Did they rape and kill Galli? The man just lost his wife to the plague and now this." Graves and McCabe exchanged glances.

"Bill and I backed out of the camp. We saw Indian bodies. From all the shooting, we have no idea how many Indians died. We didn't look for Galli. I'm calling Elko for more deputies. When they get here tomorrow, we'll go back and try to sort this all out."

Verrall Black now brought the conversation full circle. "Is there anything you want from us?" The deputies turned away from the group and quietly conferred before answering.

"An Indian war may have started tonight. What would help is if you'd all be willing to meet back here in the morning. I don't want anyone going into the village. You can

121

help us by keeping folks out of the Indian camp. We'll put two of you at each corner to keep folks out. "

"Do you want us armed?"

"Probably you'd better be, but listen here; keep them guns out of sight. Don't anyone shoot unless you're shot at first. If that happens, get the hell back to your homes and take care of your families. I'll have more men tomorrow, and I'll call the army if everything goes to hell. You are my buffer between the town and the camp. Does everybody understand?" Fifteen townsmen all signaled their agreement.

"One more thing" said Jim Graves. "We didn't take Winnemucca into custody. We figure he just wanted to mourn his daughter. If anyone sees him, stay away and come tell Bill or me. Go home now." The two deputies went inside to call for help and plan for tomorrow.

Verrall Black went to his own home and found his wife waiting inside their front door. "What's going on? Who's shooting?" He shared with his wife all he'd learned. Libby Black took her husband by the hand and led him into the dark of their parlor.

"I don't want the children to overhear anything through the bedroom wall. What do we do?"

"If something happens tonight, I'll carry Melba and you bring Doris. If it looks safe, we'll go over to the store and the extra guns. You'll take our daughters to the basement storeroom.

"If it gets bad tomorrow morning after I've gone with the committee, do the same if you can. If you can't get to the store, get the girls to the reeds along the river; hide and wait."

"Who are the men that hurt Galli?"

Verrall shook his head and repeated the names of the four men. He rose and took Libby's hand. "Go to sleep now. I'm going to stay here for a while. We'll all be fine." And with a brief kiss, he turned her towards the stairs. *I pray that's not our last kiss.* He took a shotgun from their hall closet, chambered a round and took a seat deep in the shadows.

* * *

Samuel Winnemucca passed through the dark, away from where the Griswolds died. He'd claimed responsibility for all the killings. No other band needed to suffer because they had heeded his call to stop the men who'd raped and murdered his daughter. White justice would not be gentler on an Indian who killed two whites instead of four. Samuel didn't plan to be around when morning came.

Jimmy Hokwaits was still outside the Winnemucca' wickiup. "The women are still preparing the body. Sit with me a while." Jimmy carefully laid his hand on the big man's arm, gently pushing him towards the log seats by the outside firepit.

Sitting side by side, Jimmy Hokwaits took Samuel's rifle and Samuel drew his skinning knife and began cutting off his own hair. Next he used the blade to cut two shallow gashes on each cheek. "I'll be gone as soon as her body is prepared."

Hokwaits listened silently, ready to do anything his friend asked.

"I killed two and other hunters killed two more, but I told the deputies I killed them all. Tonight you spread the word that no one else killed the whites. I have to go."

Jimmy looked back into Samuel's flat, black eyes set deep above blood-covered cheeks. His response was immediate. "I will, and when you are gone, our bands will honor Galilhai with the Salt Songs and the Bird Songs. We'll praise her beauty and I will bury her next to Pamahas?"

Samuels signaled "Yes," by a single nod.

"My animals are yours. Wait until the bands are gone and then burn everything I left behind."

123

Now it was Jimmy's turn to nod his understanding. "I'll go now. You wait to see your child." Jimmy left to find the other shooters and tell them Samuel was taking on all the white rage. With no wife nor family, the hunter had nothing to lose. This was his last, best act to protect his people whom he'd see again: if not in this world, then in the next.

When Galli's body was cleaned, dressed in her best traditional clothing, her hair combed and braided, the women quietly left. "Samuel, she is ready," and then they were gone.

Inside the wickiup, by the light of its small fire, Galilhai lay peacefully on clean deer skins. He knelt by her side and placed his hand over hers. Alone at last, Samuel shed the only tears that would ever fall. Their drops turned the ribbons of his blood a lighter shade as they ran down his cheeks. With no more tears to shed and knowing his child would sleep with her mother, Samuel collected the few things he would take into the night. He took clothing, jerky, dried Camas root, an extra knife, salt, matches and bullets for his Winchester. Out the door for the last time, he slipped into the dark and disappeared.

12. The Last Ghost Dance, October 1916

As midnight arrived, the seven shamans gathered at the base of Indian Hill. They took peyote, introduced to them years before by the tribes from the lower Southwest. The hallucinogen brought them vivid dreams, their spirit guides from the other world that would help them chart a course of action for their bands.

When the peyote had done its work, the shamans shared their visions as the first light of dawn appeared above the distant Ruby Mountain peaks. The Ghost Dance would end. Their sacred meeting place on top of Indian Hill was damaged and its power gone. Whether the power was drained by the killings or the white man's disease didn't matter now. With the magic gone, their people needed to leave this place.

The shamans went to the singers and drummers up on the hill. When the drumming and singing stopped, so did the dancers. The shamans told the people it was time to gather their bands and leave this place. Each band was to take their sick and dead away. There was much to do and reason to be gone; so said their visions.

Shelters were abandoned to the desert winds, snakes and rabbits. Clothes and cooking utensils were hurriedly packed. The bodies of the men killed in answer to Samuel Winnemucca's call were removed. Only the body of Galilhai remained in the village until she rested next to her mother, together in dreamless sleep.

* * *

At 7:00 A.M. five deputies arrived from Elko in a department Model T. Bill and Jim had coffee ready. After they filled their cups, the men used all the office chairs. The rest cleared spots and sat down on the desk tops. Jim Graves explained what they'd seen and what Samuel Winnemucca had said last night. This morning the seven of them would return to the village while the "committee men" kept the town and the Indians apart.

"Here's the deal. We could be going into a powder keg. A local Paiute, Sam Winnemucca, confessed to killing the four locals, and we're bringing out their bodies. Winnemucca said that the four raped and killed his daughter. We need to find her body. Sam is still out there somewhere. He's a professional hunter, so you need to be damn careful."

The five deputies from Elko were all tough, seasoned lawmen. There were no side-glances or doubts; they would execute Deputy Graves's plan. They drank their coffee and listened to the man in charge. The committee men were to return in another hour.

"We are going to split into two groups. Bill and four of you will bring out the bodies of the dead whites." Jim pointed at Deputy Wiley Brooks. "Wiley, you'll be with me. We'll bring out the girl's body."

Graves and McCabe noticed it immediately. The hypnotic sounds of drumming and foot stomps, together strong enough to vibrate the air, had stopped. The two men looked at one another. Graves continued, "If we can."

126

"What's that mean?" questioned Phil Gray, another of the Elko deputies. "We're the law, aren't we?"

Bill McCabe now spoke up. "Listen Phil, we've got 500 pissed off Indians out there. They have...we don't know how many guns, not to mention the guns from those four dead idiots. I sure as hell don't want the next Indian war to begin here—today." McCabe kept his eyes focused on his counterpart from Elko. "Let's do what we need to do and get out with our lives. All right?"

Gray grunted his agreement.

"One last thing," said Jim Graves. "Bill and I know Sam Winnemucca by sight, you fellas don't. Unless Bill or I see him, you just be as quiet and non-threatening as you can, notwithstanding the rifle you're each packing." Graves drained his tin cup and set it down on top of a file cabinet. "Let's go."

* * *

When the locals arrived, ready to help with keeping town and Indians apart, deputies and citizens headed out together. At the end of the last block, with the encampment in sight, Jim Graves gave directions to Verrall Black and his men. He posted pairs of men on both street corners, two to a side. He sent other men to both sets of rail tracks and the final pair to the river bank. Their orders were to keep townspeople out of the encampment. Unstated was the other face of this same coin; keep the Paiutes in.

Verrall Black stayed with Jim Graves and another Elko Deputy. With the town and encampment separated by armed men, Bill McCabe pointed the way towards the bodies for Deputy Arli Cavender and his group. All eight men stopped at the opening to the crescent horns of the camp. Before them, on both sides, the entire camp bustled with activity. Cars, trucks, horses or simple packs were being loaded at every site not already vacated.

"We'll stay here and let 'em go. A lot less risk that way and they will not take white bodies," Graves told the group. For the next hour, none of the lawmen moved.

Out of view, off to their right, Jimmy Hokwaits was keeping his promise to Samuel. He held Galilhai Winnemucca's body in his arms. A grave beside Pamahas' resting place was already prepared. Jimmy would bear his burden to the spot, and if his arms or back ached, it didn't matter. His friend's daughter would be carried to her rest, and his comfort was inconsequential

Jim Graves and the others watched the Paiute camp dissolve before their eyes. After an hour, all that remained were sage domes above hollowed desert dugouts. The lawmen shared their collective relief. They weren't going into an ambush. All that remained was collecting the dead.

Bill McCabe and his partner knew that the camp circled around the back of Indian Hill. What they'd find this morning was an unknown.

Jim Graves finally said, "Let's go. We'll meet on the backside of the hill, so we miss nothing." McCabe and four went left as Jim Graves, Wiley Brooks and Verrall Black headed right.

Verrill knew the Winnemucca wickiup. His girls had played with Galli. He himself had picked up pine nuts and deer skin gloves from Pamahas at her home. As they approached, he pointed, "There."

Jim Graves was first through the blanket-covered doorway. From long acquaintance, he knew the metallic smell of blood and it filled his nostrils now. Light came through the central smoke hole in the ceiling, while the floor near the walls remained cloaked in shadow. "Wiley, hold back the blanket. I need more light."

Graves circled the interior, checking the floor before him as he walked. Opposite the doorway, between firepit and back wall, the blood smell was intense. At his feet, a drying pool of blood stained a deerskin rug. A double-barreled shotgun leaned against the wall in front of him. He picked up the gun. Its two hammers were down, not cocked. Pushing the release lever behind the hammers, he broke open the gun's action. Both barrels were empty.

Graves carried the gun in the crook of his arm as he circled the wickiup. Wiley Brooks was still holding back the doorway cover and Verrall Black stood outside looking in.

"Somebody died here, from the amount of blood. Let's go around the outside of the wickiup and see if we see anything there," and Graves followed Wiley Brooks out back, where they found nothing to answer their questions about what had happened last night, so on they moved, continuing around the backside of the hill.

* * *

Bill McCabe and the other deputies moved past abandoned dugouts. There were still warm campfires next to rubber tire tracks where other Paiutes had camped beside their iron horses. Alerted by the fecal smell, they looked twenty yards ahead, where shapes lay low on the dirt. It was two naked bodies: Cannon and Edison.

The Indians had picked the bodies clean. Neither clothes nor guns remained. Then the bodies had become toilets. Austin Cannon lay face down in the dirt, the back of his head a bloody smashed pumpkin. Ike Edison lay on his back, shot in the face. His one remaining eye stared fixedly into the sky. Blue-bottle flies swarmed into the air when McCabe threatened their feast. Arli Cavender bolted away, collapsed to his knees, and puked onto the dirt.

"It's Cannon and Edison. Let's move on," directed McCabe.

The four deputies moved a few steps away and waited for Cavender. Not far ahead lay Art and Tom Griswold, both picked clean and similarly defiled. Their bodies suggested a gun battle. Each man was dead from multiple wounds to their legs and torsos. Bill McCabe spoke the brothers' names before ordering, "We keep moving." On the five went to the far side of the hill. They found no dead Indians, only pools of dried blood and drag marks suggesting that at least four Indians had fallen.

They stopped as Jim Graves and his group came into sight. He'd passed the shotgun to Verrall Black. Brevity marked both groups' reports. They found no Indian bodies, especially not the body of Galilhai Winnemucca. But the scene supported her Father's claim that she'd been the victim of violence. McCabe described the four white bodies, stripped and defiled.

"The Paiutes usually lift scalps as trophies, but what they did to the bodies..." McCabe's eyes closed as he shook his head.

"That was their ultimate sign of scorn for the men. Paiutes wouldn't do that unless they thought the four were evil and below contempt." Verrall Black was the speaker and a long silence followed until Bill McCabe spoke again to his group.

"Two of you go back and wait with each set of bodies. We are not taking anyone back to town in that condition, I don't care what they might have done." He looked at Jim Graves, confirmed that they were of one mind.

"Verrall, would you be willing to take Wiley to town and come back with tarps and a cart for hauling the bodies? One more thing, don't any of you say a damn word about how we found the bodies. Understood?"

"Yup," came back the answers.

Verrall nudged Wiley Brooks, "Let's go"

Now Bill McCabe turned to the five Elko deputies. "I will not ask any of you to wash shit off of dead bodies. If you can help me get them on tarps and down to the river, I'll take care of that chore myself. Are you good with that?" McCabe hadn't mentioned Arli Cavender's puking after seeing the first set of bodies. Cavender spoke up, "Yes, we will."

130

Deeth deputies Graves and McCabe stood their ground, finally able to talk. Now they could speculate openly. "I think the Indians took all their dead, so who knows if she was raped and killed," offered Bill.

"From the blood I saw, someone died in there, in Samuel's house. The shotgun I brought back came from inside Sam's wickiup. Those fellas who were all about disarming the Paiutes sure as hell didn't. So why were they in Samuel's house, then?"

Bill showed his agreement with everything Jim pointed out.

"And I'll tell you something else. Sam didn't shoot the Griswolds. There were too many bullet holes in 'em. Sam is a better shot than that. Look at Cannon and Edison; that's how Sam kills."

* * *

Four bodies, all cleansed in the river, arrived back in town. Telephones had come to Deeth, but not a mortician.

Jim Graves pulled Black aside. "Verrall, would you be willing to tell the wives their husbands' bodies are at my office?"

"I will."

"You know the condition of the bodies. Tell the widows I'll arrange to transport their husbands to Stiffel's Funeral Home in Elko, if they want. I'd just as soon that their women didn't have to see them, especially Cannon and Edison."

"I understand. I'll do my best." Without hesitation Verrall added, "I'll take them in for you, Jim. We might need my truck, depending on how many bodies are going to Elko."

Jim Graves shook the merchant's hand, and they parted. Besides ten deaths from polio and fifty active cases, the town now had to deal with five murders.

Graves found Phineas Franklin in his office behind the barroom. The forty-year-old saloon owner, now gray and bent, sat with a shot glass in hand behind his desk with his door closed. Franklin's eyes lifted when the deputy entered. His expression didn't change. He poured a second drink, slid it across the desktop and went back to examining the amber liquor in his glass. Jim Graves didn't take the offered seat or the drink. Instead, he leaned on the desk top and stared fixedly at Franklin.

"I saw you go into the camp. Tell me about it. Your plan—their instruction—and how your idea turned to shit and got them all killed."

"We only wanted to take their guns. That was all." Franklin's words were slurred. Graves reached across the desk and took the drink from Phin's hand. He'd get no more from Franklin now. Having removed a shotgun from the murder site, Jim was sure he'd just heard a self-serving justification. *What a lying son-of-a-bitch and a coward to boot.* Graves set Phin's drink back down, slid his own untouched whisky across the desk and left the office.

* * *

Verrall Black went straight home from the Sheriff's Office. He needed his wife's help to be there when he made the notifications. Swearing his wife to eternal silence he shared with her what he'd seen.

"They killed Galli and probably raped her first. Her body was already gone, but we saw the blood, and there was a lot of it. Samuel vanished but not before telling what they'd done to his daughter. Then he admitted to killing all of 'em."

Verrall and Libby needed to convince two of the widows not to look at their husband's bodies, leaving unsaid why they shouldn't. They would call other family friends to sit with the bereaved women after Verrall and Libby delivered their news. All four bodies were headed into Stiffel's. Verrall told the widows that he'd get the bodies to Elko, and Libby volunteered to drive their truck so her husband was available if Jim Graves needed any more assistance.

13. Revenge

Samuel could live off the land. Food and shelter were plentiful if you knew where to look, and he did. The hunter knew every deer track and trail for miles.

Looking out through the pale yellow light of sunrise, he watched what was happening back in Deeth. There was time enough to move on into the wild later. Before he departed, there was the last man whom Samuel had yet to visit: the tall one who abandoned his friends.

Samuel watched from the top of Indian Hill, the last place he'd be expected. This should have been the start of day four of the five-day Ghost Dance. He figured that so soon after the killings, few people knew about his confession. The town and the law expected him to run rather than wait. Any efforts to track him were still being organized at nine in the morning after the killings. Off to his right, he could see smoke rising from the village. *Jimmy is keeping his promise, burning the death house. My daughter will be at her mother's side by now.*

Samuel moved down to the river's edge, screened by a reed wall from the buildings, until he was behind Phineas Franklin's saloon. Leaving his rifle among the reeds, he crept forward with only Austin Cannon's pistol tucked in his belt. He knew the layout of the building from having delivered venison steaks to the cooks. He also knew which door led to Franklin's office, where he collected his pay for each delivery. Still unseen at the back door, Samuel removed his shoes to enter unseen and unheard.

The kitchen was empty. He stood there listening before entering the short length of hallway that connected to the office. Nothing came to his ear as he moved along the wall to the closed office door. Turning the knob, he pushed the door open, its hinges blessedly quiet.

Phin Franklin was inside. The tall man lay face down on his desktop, a half-empty whiskey bottle to his right and an empty glass on its side to his left. Samuel slipped in and closed the door. He could smell the whisky oozing from Franklin's pores as the drunk snored, his forehead and nose touching the desk surface.

From behind Phin's chair, Samuel first poured another shot from bottle to glass. He took the pistol from his belt and placed it on the desk top. Now, with one palm on the slumping man's right shoulder, he lifted Franklin back to a seated position. Franklin moaned and then snorted a half-swallowed cough as his eyes opened to half-mast. Samuel put his mouth next to Phin's ear and murmured, "Shoo-shoo," in a low, gentle, reassuring tone as he placed the refilled whisky glass in Franklin's hand. "Take another drink now, then you can sleep again."

Franklin brought the glass to his lips, swallowing and spilling equal amounts. But he did not try to identify the unknown voice or hand on his shoulder.

Samuel took the empty glass from the drunk's hand and replaced it with the pistol, an index finger on the trigger. He guided the gun to Franklin's head. "Sleep now," and Sam's own finger forced the index finger to squeeze the trigger.

After the shot rang out, Franklin's head and hand dropped to the desk top. Blood began spreading from the bullet hole in his temple. A black circle of burned powder ringed the hole, testifying to contact between muzzle and skin. Samuel was out the door and through the kitchen, still unseen and unheard. At the creek bank, he reclaimed his rifle and left Deeth forever.

* * *

Belle Robinson had filled the vacancy created by the death of Lottie Loomis. Phineas Franklin took a special interest in the young red-headed entrepreneur, and she reciprocated his interest. Employing her best feminine wiles, Belle had made Phin feel himself the king he aspired to be.

The ladies slept late, after long nights of providing comfort and companionship to the town's men. Belle, Minnie, and Mabel enjoyed their "lady time" together each morning. They had their brunch daily from 10 to 11 A.M. in a warm corner of the kitchen. Minnie and Mabel were well aware that Belle had her eye on becoming Mrs. Phineas Franklin.

"Is he a big man, darling?" Mabel asked, a broad smile on her lips.

Smiling, Belle shook her head. "Small hands," and the three ladies burst into fits of laughter at the coded answer. Franklin had not been well endowed below the waist.

When their ritual brunch concluded, Belle got up. "Well, it's time for me to do my daily chore. I have a cane to polish." Another coded answer brought more smiles to the other two working girls.

Belle passed from kitchen through the hall and opened Phin's office door. Franklin's long torso sprawled across his desk top. A pistol was clutched in his left hand. Blood leaking from his skull darkened the far side of his desk

Shit! Now what am I going to do?

Belle had to alert the authorities, true. But first, she emptied the stash Phin kept in a hollowed-out book, shelved across the room. She removed the bills and tucked them into her cleavage. From the open office doorway, she let out her best theatrical distress scream and waited to see if anyone took her bait.

Two screams later, Sarge the sweeper lumbered down the hall to find the three distraught women staring into his boss's office.

"I've seen worse." He turned back out of the doorway and headed down the hall. "I'll go tell the sheriff."

* * *

Both Jim Graves and Bill McCabe inspected the scene in Franklin's office. They found neither the footprints of an intruder nor signs of a struggle. Jim had seen Phineas the previous day and the tall man was well into his cups then. Nothing suggested anything other than the suicide of a man finally confronting the damage he'd inflicted on the town. As Bill McCabe closed the door to the murder scene, their investigation concluded, he commented to his partner, "Well at least he finally did the right thing."

14. The Renegade

Jim Graves had phoned a summary of events to his boss in Elko. They'd arranged road blocks outside of Elko and Wells, hoping to stop Sam Winnemucca. The five deputies sent from Elko blocked the road north to Wells.

Graves offered to send one man with Libby Black on her drive to Stiffel's, but she declined the offer. South and west from Deeth, the thirty-five miles to Elko should take Libby only one hour to drive. Portions of the road were now blacktopped, and those sections awaiting improvement were graveled. The highway and one or both sets of rail tracks ran parallel. The four bodies, each wrapped in a separate tarp, lay side by side on the truck bed between its low wooden sideboards. Another tarp covering all four bodies was secured to hooks at the corners.

Samuel watched the truck approach from his resting place up on the railway berm, recognizing the 'Deeth Mercantile' logo painted on the doors. He needed help to put distance between himself and his killing grounds. He got up, jogged to the side of the road and showed himself to the driver. Libby Black pulled over and stopped.

Knowing that Samuel was the admitted killer of the men who'd invaded his village didn't change her mind. *Those men who'd violated his home and raped and killed his daughter deserved to die.* Samuel stood silently at the passenger-side door, waiting for Libby's response. She was good people, and he'd slip off into the desert if she wasn't able to help.

"There is a roadblock between here and Elko. What can I do to help?" asked Libby.

"I'm going into the Rubies behind Lamoille Canyon. I'll skirt Elko and head up east toward Lamoille and into the mountains. The Te-Moak band at Spring Creek will help me. Can you drive me closer to Elko?"

Libby nodded. "We don't know where the roadblock is set up. It would be best if you hide under the tarp, between the bodies. That way you can't be seen from outside. I'm sorry to ask you to ride near those evil men."

Samuel climbed up into the truck bed. He crawled over the first tarped corpse and pushed it toward the rear, making room for himself to lie down. Libby put the truck back in gear and continued toward Elko with her grisly load.

They'd traveled thirty-two miles when ahead on the long flat stretch a collection of vehicles appeared and loomed larger as she neared. Two sheriff's cars parked nose to nose blocked the way. Six deputies with rifles stood behind the improvised barricade. Libby slowed and came to a stop in front of them.

Four deputies, their rifles at port arms, approached the truck, two shooters per side. Verrall and Libby Black were well known to the Elko County Sheriffs. Two deputies recognized Mrs. Black from Deeth, and they gestured that the other two could lower their rifles as Alvin St. Claire walked up to the driver's door.

"Hello Mrs. Black. Jim Graves told us you'd be bringing the bodies to Stiffel's."

Deputy John Armstrong, now long recovered from being wounded by Leonard Fristoe, had also recognized Libby Black. He leaned into the cab from the passenger's door. Comfortable that she was not being held at gunpoint by a killer hiding on the cab floor, he smiled an "all clear" signal to Deputy St. Claire.

The other two deputies surveyed the sideboards and the tied-down tarp. Both men walked to the back of the truck and looked in before nodding their "all clear."

"Did you have any problems on the way down?"

"No problems, and this is a load I'll be happy to get off our truck."

As the four deputies walked away, Libby called out a question. "Alvin, is there another block between here and town?"

"No, just us."

She smiled. "Oh good, the sooner I'm done with this, the better, especially since it's warming up." She restarted the truck as the two cars up ahead moved aside for her to pass.

On she and her hidden passenger went, until Libby knew Elko would come into view over the next rise. Alone on the highway, she pulled over and stopped.

Samuel emerged from his hiding place. Afraid of being seen by an unexpected passer-by, he immediately set off southeast towards the Ruby Mountains and Lamoille Canyon.

Libby sat watching him go. When he was well into the surrounding sage, Samuel turned back, raised his arm in a final goodbye, and disappeared. Libby drove the last two miles to Stiffel's and left her cargo.

* * *

Elko County Coroner Charles Mabbutt, a lawyer by trade, gave a cursory inspection to the four bodies, sufficient for him to rule the cause of death as "by gunshot" in each case. Mabbutt watched as a mortuary assistant at Stiffel's cut open the bullet tracks and removed the slugs from the bodies of the Griswold brothers.

Turning next to the Cannon corpse, they found that no cuts were needed. The assistant plunged a gloved finger into the cold goo that had once been skull and brain. The rifle bullet which had taken Cannon's life had also exploded his skull. The final bath in the river allowed the slug to slip away.

"I can't find the slug. I'm guessing it fell out." Reluctant to don a glove and check for himself, Mabbutt shrugged and then moved on to Edison's body.

Ike Edison had died last, shot twice. Stopped by a bullet to the back, he'd died from the shot in the face. The soft lead slugs used to bring down deer, bear or lions had done their worst. The two pieces of lead removed from Edison's body

140

were deformed and no longer recognizable as bullets. Mabbutt had the slugs washed and placed in small evidence boxes, one per body, with the name of the deceased recorded on the box lid.

* * *

Samuel Winnemucca stayed clear of Elko, lying off in the distance. Flat sage country changed to low rolling hills, slowly rising as he moved east towards the Rubies. Five miles east of Elko sat the settlement of Spring Creek. Just north of town, ten Te-Moak wickiups clustered along the banks of Huntington Creek. The Te-Moaks had been dancing the Ghost Dance just hours before. Every member of the band had heard Samuel's cry for help with the white intruders who'd savaged and killed his daughter.

The ground rose slowly from 7,200 feet at Elko to 8,000 at Spring Creek and to over 9,000 at the entrance to Lamoille Canyon. The back of the three-mile-deep glacier-carved canyon rose sharply to over 10,000 feet in a scant 3 miles.

It was late October now, and the mountain tops were already dusted with snow.

Samuel knew he'd need a heavy coat and boots to survive even a summer night at the top of the canyon, let alone the winter, with spring many months away. His destination was the chain of seven lakes that dotted the rocky peaks above the tree line behind Lamoille Canyon. Heavy snow was already visible on the top of 11,400 foot Ruby Dome. Unlike the heat of the valley floor, the nights in the high Rubies were often below freezing even in the summer, and possibly below zero on any other day.

John Wewa, the band's shaman and a renowned mystic, had been a principal organizer of the dancing. John's son, Hiram, lost his life to the Griswold brothers' gunfire. The old man watched Samuel approach and waved for the renegade hunter to join him. "Sit, brother." He raised a woven basket holding pine nuts, jerky and dried apple rings from his lap. "Here, eat. Water or sage tea?"

Samuel took the basket, nodding his thanks. "Tea, Puhagim," Samuel used the honorific Paiute title for a revered shaman. Wewa half-turned and called to unseen figures inside his wickiup, "Juanita, tea, por favor."

John knew Samuel Winnemucca had shouldered the responsibility for killing all four of the white men. They sat side by side on the log bench outside the wickiup. Neither man spoke as they waited for the tea. When two tin cups appeared, Samuel thanked the silent Juanita.

"She is my daughter-in-law. The whites killed her husband back in Deeth. Her heart and mind aren't yet right."

"I'm sorry." Samuel exhaled and his head slumped forward as he realized the inadequacy of his words, or any words. Overcome by his own loss, he'd not checked the other bands and tallied their cost for joining his fight.

"She's not Indian. A Mexican girl Hiram met in Elko. She was a good wife, but she doesn't understand the bonds of our bands. She suffers the loss of her man at night in her empty bed. Their only child, my grandson, has the white man's disease. It will leave him lame, if he survives. She has much to deal with. Please forgive her." And the men went silent again. When Samuel finally raised his head, John's eyes were upon him. It was time for him to make his request.

"Puhagim, I lost my wife to the white man's plague and now they've taken my daughter. I am headed up into the lake county behind the big canyon. The whites will come after me, so I cannot stay here. I can feed myself off the deer and trout, but I need other things: winter boots, a heavy coat, blankets, matches, hooks and line."

Samuel paused, reaching into his pants pocket. He removed a thick fold of paper money and passed it uncounted to the old mystic. "These things must come from stores. Will you help me?"

John Wewa nodded. He would see that the renegade hunter got the help he needed. "Noon in two days you will find someone waiting along the creek at the mouth of the big canyon." The old man put a hand down on the log bench. With the remaining strength in his two legs and one arm, he managed to push himself up. "Wait" and he disappeared into the shadows of the wickiup.

Pushing the door blanket cover aside, John stepped back into the noontime sun and passed over a bulging gingham bag. "Take this now."

Samuel held eye contact with the mystic as he took the sack. "Thank you."

"You and my son are both honorable men. Every old man needs an honorable son. Go, my son."

* * *

Juanita Wewa-Contreras was the oldest child from a prosperous ranching family in the south end of the Ruby Valley. The handsome, well-spoken Paiute, Hiram Wewa, had immediately smitten Juanita. Her family, who'd been in Nevada for over 100 years, thought the match unconventional, but Hiram won them over. As the only son of the local Paiute spiritual leader, his status within the Indian community was considerable.

Life in a Paiute wickiup was a world away from her Father's rancho. Still, the love she received in trade for inconvenience was a bargain Juanita didn't regret. When their son, Joaquin, came into their lives, Hiram built them a two-room cabin between the Te-Moak village and Spring Creek.

When seven-year-old Joaquin contracted the white man's illness, Juanita prayed to both the Virgin and to the Great Spirit of the Paiutes. She embraced the Ghost Dance as Joaquin's salvation. Now, she found herself with no one to pray to, no husband, and no help for her child, struggling mightily to breathe.

Juanita was not yet ready to face an empty cabin and empty bed. She had brought Joaquin to her husband's parents' home. For how long, she had no idea, but doting grandparents provided her help with tending to Joaquin and comfort at the moment of her widowhood.

John Wewa prepared a list of items Samuel needed. "Juanita, my child, would you take our horse into town and buy these things for me, por favor?"

"Si, padre." The old man passed over his list: clothing, food, and other supplies. She'd overheard John's conversation with the renegade hunter, the cause of her husband's death. She also knew when and where Samuel would receive the goods. Spring Creek lacked a store, so Juanita rode into Elko. Her first stop in town was the Sheriff's Office. She had information to trade if and only if she could secure white man's help for her son.

* * *

"I want to talk to the Sheriff about the four men killed in Deeth." When pressed about why, Juanita wouldn't say. "I will only talk to the Sheriff." Her unwillingness to speak to the first white face in uniform got her ignored, so she played the only card that a Chicana had left to play.

"Please tell Sheriff Escuraga that Juanita Contreras, daughter of Aurelio Contreras, wishes to see him." The

Contreras family had a ranching operation outside of Elko. Her family name and the Sheriff's might get her in; and it did.

Sheriff Abarran Escuraga stood behind his desk when Juanita entered his office. A fourth generation Nevada Basque, Escuraga knew the Contreras family. He also knew the Wewa family. Juanita Wewa-Contreras would always have his attention when she wished. She mentioned her husband's death and her son's illness.

"I'm so sorry about Hiram's being killed, and about little Joaquin's condition. The polio is here too, and none of the doctors have a cure. The state is setting up a special place to treat the afflicted; rocking beds, iron lung machines, mineral baths and people to make braces for their legs. It seems to be all we can do, but I assure you we are doing all we can."

After the obligatory exchange of pleasantries, her business with Sheriff Escuraga commenced.

"I may have heard something about the fugitive Winnemucca."

Escuraga leaned forward.

"If I were to help you find him, can you help me get Joaquin into this special hospital?"

He nodded. "Perhaps."

"No perhaps about it. I will only tell if you promise this to me."

The sheriff stalled. "Juanita, do you have other business in town?"

She replied she did, but did not explain the business.

"If you come back here in...say, two hours, I will have an answer for you."

Thus agreed, they separated for now.

Sheriff Escuraga first called the Elko County Prosecuting Attorney Donald Miles, then he called the Chief Judge, asking both for an urgent meeting. Over the phone he would only reveal that they'd be discussing a promising lead in the Deeth murders. The three gathered in the judge's chambers.

146

"Sheriff, you asked for the meeting, so the floor is yours," said the Prosecuting Attorney.

"Juanita Contreras, Aurelio's daughter, came to see me. She didn't say it, but she knows where Sam Winnemucca is. She wants to trade the information for getting her boy Joaquin into the polio care wing at the state hospital." The Sheriff then got up and began to leave the meeting. "This is not my business. I'll be outside."

"Jeez, make the deal. Promise her anything she wants. That son-of-a-bitch killed four whites," said Miles. The prosecutor could barely contain his excitement at the thought of a show trial that would make his political career.

The judge listened to the interchange. "If you think this is the best move, Donald. Tell Mrs. Wewa I'll call the governor. He'll call the hospital superintendent and arrange bedspace for the kid." Judge Wells sat back in his leather-covered chair, thinking.

"One more question. Donald, are you sure you can make the case? You have a confession but no physical evidence to support it. That's a risk. You know that I'll need more than a confession alone: evidence—proof—something. You better be God-damn sure you can convict this guy."

Without thought or hesitation Miles' answer emerged. "Make the deal."

"I'll call the Governor and see if he can pull some strings: sneak the little half breed in the back door. Personally I doubt it, but what matters is what Juanita believes," confided Judge Wells.

As the sheriff left the Judge's chambers, Miles cornered Escuraga in the hallway. "Your men better find me the Indian's gun, or we're sunk."

"Correction. You're sunk, Mr. Prosecutor," said Sheriff Escuraga.

* * *

147

When Juanita returned to the Sheriff's office, he escorted her next door to the county courthouse and into the chambers of Judge Wells, but Escuraga stayed outside.

Prosecutor Miles and Judge Ronald Wells were awaiting her arrival. Both men stood when she entered. Judge Wells motioned to a chair. "Please sit."

Miles laid it out. "Juanita, you have a deal. If you tell me where Winnemucca is, Joaquin will have a place in the new polio wing at the State Hospital in Sparks. He'll get the best care possible. If he needs leg braces or some such later on, that will be provided too."

Both men stared at the widow. She returned their stares, searching one face at a time for hints of honesty or duplicity.

Finally, Prosecutor Miles broke the silence. "Juanita, do we have a deal?"

"Yes."

Juanita checked the two faces again. Unfortunately, the prosecutor and Judge hid their lies very well. They knew the governor would be unwilling to promise a bed to a half-breed child when so many white children needed help. She'd received an empty promise that would later be denied if she was foolish enough to make such a claim.

Abarran met her outside the Judge's chambers and walked her back to his own office. She told the Sheriff about the supplies that would be delivered to Samuel Winnemucca. "He will be along the creek at the mouth of Lamoille Canyon tomorrow, noon."

Later that afternoon, the sheriff arranged his ambush. Eight deputies would be waiting when the renegade Winnemucca showed up. The men were told, "We want him alive for trial and we want his gun. Get them both."

"Do we arrest whoever he meets, or let them go?" asked Chief Deputy Sheriff Clint White, who would lead the posse.

"Arrest them too."

* * *

Juanita had already filled her Father-in-law's list, so she made it back to the village outside Spring Creek by the early afternoon. The old man motioned for her to leave the goods in the packs. Without a car or truck in their village, it was a two-hour horse trip to keep the noon rendezvous at Lamoille Canyon.

"Mi hija, I am too old to do this. I need you to meet Samuel tomorrow. Will you do that for me?"

"Si padre, I will. When and where?" Even though she had already overheard, pretending to find out now would make her appear blameless after Samuel was arrested or shot down. She hid a momentary qualm...but mother love trumped family loyalty. She would do what she had to do.

16. Betrayed

Samuel Winnemucca spent his first night in Lamoille Canyon. He'd wait low in the canyon until he had clothes and supplies before traveling up into the lake country above.

Only 100 yards wide, the canyon floor rose steadily along its three-mile length. Pure water flowed in a quiet stream that emerged from the ground at the canyon's head. Its banks were lush with grass and skunk cabbage below the towering granite cliffs on one side. The other bank moved from grass to a belt of aspen trees, filling the slope up to the base of similar cliffs on the other side.

Samuel camped at the foot of the cliff behind the screen of aspens. Dry branches made a small smokeless fire. Without either his wife or daughter, he felt himself no more alone over his small fire than he would have been alone in his wickiup. While he waited for his noon meeting and the supplies he needed, planning filled his mind.

I'll look for a cave or rock shelter above the lakes. I should probably keep several camps and move often. If the winter is too hard, I'll come down behind Angel Lake. I can see north to Wells and south to Deeth from there.

He had no other thoughts about a future. There would be time enough to plan while the winter snow kept pursuers away and bottled him up. With the sun as his only clock, Samuel waited for the white-hot sphere to rise to its full height and bring light to both sides of the steep canyon cliffs. Then he'd move down to the meeting site.

The aspens that gave him cover also shortened his field of vision. A mile outside the mouth of the canyon, eight deputies approached on foot. Deputy White knew when, but he didn't know exactly where along the creek or from which side to expect Winnemucca. He was after an outdoorsman who made a living with his rifle and had now used it to kill four men.

Outside of Elko and away from their bosses, White briefed his men. "Our orders are to take Winnemucca alive, and we will if we can. That will be up to him. Whoever brings him supplies, the same rules apply. Alive if we can. But we all go home tonight."

Half a mile from the canyon's mouth the eight men ducked down at the sight of Juanita Wewa, riding alone and leading a pack horse towards the meeting site. The second horse carried four supply bags draped in twos across its packsaddle. Deputy White signaled his men to follow Juanita as she led them to their prey.

Samuel's camp was a quarter mile inside the canyon's mouth. There were no landmarks for his noon meeting: not a building, a junction, or a confluence of waters. It was somewhere along a 100-foot stretch of creek wherever the bank and brush allowed. He'd cross to the creek from his camp and follow the winding water down to the canyon mouth.

Where the canyon opened to the high desert, small stands of willows hugged the creek. He'd wait under the cover of the trees where he, John Wewa and Hiram had fished. He and John knew the spot, but if the 70-year-old was sending another person, Samuel must spot the messenger.

Juanita came into sight as Samuel watched the trail from town. He stepped out from his cover and raised an arm to draw her attention. She saw his signal and waived back. The deputies also saw the signal. As arranged, four men circled above, putting themselves between Winnemucca and the shelter of the canyon. Below the meeting spot, the other four deputies waited. On White's signal they would close in and arrest Winnemucca if they could, or kill him if he resisted.

White waited until Juanita disappeared into the small stand of willows. He let the pair begin unloading supplies. When their hands were full, he closed his noose. The eight armed men encircling Juanita and Samuel all stepped forward at once. Eight rifle barrels sighted down on the pair.

"Samuel, Juanita, drop any weapons you have and put your hands up. If you don't, we'll shoot you where you stand." White waited to see if anyone was about to die.

Samuel had laid his rifle down to deal with the supplies. Seeing only two deputies at first, he hesitated and began inching towards his weapon.

"Don't," said a voice from somewhere behind him. Turning brought two more rifle-pointing deputies into sight. When the final four lawmen broke from cover among the willows across the creek, Samuel raised his arms high.

They marched Samuel in hand irons down the road to the cluster of three sheriff's department cars parked at the final intersection between the canyon and Elko. Also in irons, Juanita Wewa-Contreras was mounted on her horse and led along while the pack horse trailed behind. *I guess they want to put on a show for him by arresting me,* she thought.

* * *

Word of Samuel's arrest reached the Deeth deputies that same afternoon. Jim Graves shared the news with the four widows and Verrall Black. The news quickly spread. The town already knew about Galli's rape, the four dead men and Phin Franklin's apparent suicide. Three separate conversations took place that evening.

Jim Graves and Bill McCabe both believed Samuel Winnemucca hadn't killed the Griswolds. The two had walked away from Phineas Franklin's plan to confiscate the Paiute's guns. Jim had seen the blood in Samuel's wickiup and found the shotgun still in the wickiup, casting doubt on Cannon and Edison's motive. In Jim's mind, the blood on the wickiup floor made them guilty of rape and murder.

"I can see why he killed the two." Bill McCabe agreed with his partner's conclusion. "But I still don't think he killed the Griswolds. Those two lost their lives to some piss-poor shooting."

* * *

Over coffee inside the Union Cattle Company office Wilson Finch, Shorty Roberts and Virgil Comstock had a different thought. "Sam's one of the finest men I ever met. He is not a cold-blooded killer," asserted Virgil.

"I've never heard anyone say a nasty word about the man," added Wilson Finch.

Shorty Roberts dropped his feet to the floor from the corner of Finch's desk. "Nhe nust' nave veen nout of nis nead."

Virgil and Wilson both looked at Shorty. The idea of temporary insanity made sense.

"Shorty, I believe you've got a point. It was all too much for the man to bear, and he just snapped." Wilson Finch went even further. "He'll need an excellent lawyer to convince a white jury how a Paiute's killing four men could be anything other than cold-blooded murder."

"He'd lost his wife to a terrible death and then finds his only daughter raped and murdered. Crazy nor not, I'd have killed the sons-of-bitches if it had been me." said Virgil.

* * *

Verrall and Libby Black sat at their kitchen table the night after Samuel's arrest, trying to understand how and why things were going to hell so fast.

"Verrall, we've known Samuel and Pam for twenty years. The man is just not a killer." When he nodded in agreement, Libby continued. "We need to do what we can to help him."

"I'll make some calls and see about getting him an attorney," Verrall told his wife.

None of the three separate conversations were over yet. In the days to come, the three shared perspectives merged into a course of action.

* * *

After Juanita's arrest, Sheriff Escuraga visited her in her jail. "You'll be in here today, then Prosecutor Miles will say he didn't have enough evidence to charge you and you'll be released. That way it doesn't mark you as our informant."

The following morning Donald Miles surveyed the physical evidence; Winnemucca's Winchester rifle and three sets of slugs. Sheriff Escuraga sat off to the side, watching Miles and Coroner Mabbutt.

"How come there are only three boxes of slugs? There were four victims," Miles asked.

"I couldn't find a slug in what it left of Austin Cannon's head. Sorry. "

"Which ones came from Edison?"

The coroner slid forward one of the three paper boxes. Miles examined the two scraps of lead that had once been bullets. "What the hell am I supposed to do with these? We can't match this garbage to Winnemucca's gun."

Mabbutt remained silent and gave a 'don't blame me' shrug.

Prosecutor Miles slid the final two boxes across his desk top and let go a sigh of relief when he saw recognizable slugs in each box. Coroner Mabbutt leaned across the desk, touching first one box and then the other as he identified their contents. "Art Griswold—Tom Griswold."

Next, the prosecutor turned to the sheriff. "Abarran, how quick can you match these to Winnemucca's rifle?"

"I'll have my man look today." The sheriff stepped over to the desk. He picked up the two evidence boxes and then tucked the rifle in the crook of his elbow. "These slugs look good. He should be able to do a comparison."

"Finally I get some good news for a change!" With that, the sheriff and coroner departed, leaving Prosecutor Miles to plan his future political trajectory after convicting Samuel Winnemucca.

Samuel Winnemucca and Juanita Wewa-Contreras made their initial court appearances later that day. Miles had leaked word of the renegade's arrest. The court room gallery was appropriately filled with reporters from four papers and the simply curious, all wanting to hear the charges.

"Four counts of murder, your Honor."

Judge Wells spoke from the bench. "Mister Winnemucca, do you have an attorney?"

The defendant shook his head.

The Judge nodded. "I will have my clerk call around to our local attorneys and find you representation."

Samuel made no response. *Why bother? They already decided they're going to hang me, attorney or not.*

"The court will continue your case for entry of a plea until counsel represents you."

"Your honor, if I may."

"Mr. Miles."

"The prosecution is not charging Mrs. Wewa-Contreras. We have learned she was unaware of defendant Winnemucca's status as a fugitive, or even aware of his crimes." Knowing the back-story to Samuel's arrest, Judge Wells had expected as much.

"Mrs. Wewa-Contreras, you are free to go. On behalf of Elko County, the court apologizes for your inconvenience."

Juanita nodded to the court, turned and walked out of the court room with both her father and father-in-law.

17. Search

Prosecutor Miles told Judge Wells' Clerk that his office would track down an attorney for Sam Winnemucca. Miles himself undertook the job of calling every attorney in Elko and warning each one away from representing the Indian killer. His one exception was newly minted attorney Benjamin Parker. Parker's unimpressive physical appearance, short and balding, belied his sharp legal mind.

"Mr. Parker, this is Donald Miles calling." Chatting up the legal newcomer, the prosecutor offered him the job. "I was new to the law once, and I thought you might like the work?"

Even Benjamin Parker, so green that he still grew whenever the sun came out, knew he was being offered a losing case. But a losing case was better than no case, and any publicity was better than no publicity. He took the job.

By the second day after Samuel's arrest, all of Verrall Black's contacts with Elko attorneys had done no good. He got a litany of excuses why each could not handle the Winnemucca defense. That afternoon Verrall told Libby his efforts were fruitless. He'd take her out for a cold beer while they tried to come up with another option.

It a corner of the Cannon saloon, the Blacks found Deputies Graves and McCabe sharing a table with three friends from the cattle company. Jim Graves motioned the couple to join them at their table. Shorty Roberts and Virgil Comstock pulled over extra chairs and the five men spread out, making room for the new arrivals.

Verrall Black was first to share his failed efforts on Samuel's behalf. Each subgroup then shared their thoughts about the case against Samuel.

"We learned today that Samuel is represented by the new guy, Benjamin Parker," said Bill McCabe. "They've put the arraignment off for a few days so Parker can meet his client. Miles has bullets being matched to Sam's rifle. That's good for the prosecution, but not for Sam."

Verrall Black shook his head in frustration before speaking. "Hell, I called every attorney in Elko and they all made some excuse why they couldn't represent Sam. Too busy, scheduling conflicts, vacations, retiring; you name it, and I heard it."

"But you didn't call this Parker fella?" asked Wilson Finch.

"I didn't even know he'd hung out his shingle."

"Samuel is going to need a real cracker jack attorney, not some fella who's learning as he goes along. I just don't know where to find a good lawyer or how he'd get paid." Jim Graves lowered his head to study the table top, looking for answers that had eluded him so far. Deputies Graves and McCabe had the inside track on information but not ideas.

"Nif Namlet ndoes a snory, na naper snends nan nattorney."

Six sets of eyes shifted to fix on Shorty Roberts.

Virgil was first to see the potential in his harelipped friend's idea. "By gosh, he's right. Hamlet's paper can afford the best attorney, and it's a great sequel to their series about the Jarbidge robbery. Think of it. 'Heroic father accused of murdering his daughter's rapist.' Maybe, 'Locals deny representation to Indian hero.' Or, 'Father of kidnapped Indian Princess accused of murder.' This almost writes itself."

The six sets of eyes switched to Virgil.

"This could work," commented Jim Graves. Heads nodded in agreement.

"Shorty and I guided Harry and Jack. I'll call him tomorrow."

* * *

"*New York World*," announced the operator. "How may I direct your call?"

"Harry Hamlet, please..."

"Hamlet."

"Harry, this is Virgil Comstock from Deeth. I've got a story for you. Actually a series, like you did last time."

"Hey Virgil, it's good to hear from you. Are all my friends out there doing all right?" From the pause that followed, Harry figured they were not. "Why don't you tell me what you've got."

Virgil Comstock summarized what had happened in Deeth. He started with the raging polio epidemic. He mentioned Pamahas Winnemucca's death to the virus and how it had also touched the Black family. Harry understood the fear and class distrust the incurable disease had brought to New York City. He could imagine the same fear, blaming, and suspicion powerfully affecting the small Nevada town.

When Virgil described the Ghost Dance, Harry immediately connected it to the Wounded Knee Massacre of 1890. In the actions of Phineas Franklin and the rape and murder of Galli Winnemucca, he recognized the collection of heinous events as a saleable story line for Joe Pulitzer's readers. With all the background now laid out for the reporter, Virgil moved on to the big ask.

"The County Prosecutor is looking to ride Samuel's case to a political career. The trial will be quick and dirty. For some strange reason, the only local attorney who'll touch the case is a brand new fella. Samuel would be his first criminal case."

Virgil let the implied lynching sink in. "Shorty thought your boss might spring for a talented attorney. You and Jack can do pictures and daily reports on this whole dirty business and cover the trial in Elko. What do you think?"

The phone line was quiet for a full minute as Harry Hamlet weighed the opportunity and how he could sell the idea of another series to his bosses.

"Virgil, I understand the urgency of getting a first rate attorney for Sam. The series about the Jarbidge Robbery, Galli's kidnapping, and the hidden loot was a success for the paper. I'll pitch another series to the bosses today and get back to you as soon as I can. Where do you want me to call?" Comstock provided the phone numbers for both the Union Cattle Company office and Verrall and Libby Black's home.

"I have one last question. When is Sam's next court date?"

"Four days from now, for entry of his plea."

* * *

Harry Hamlet's bosses were firm believers in the '*If it bleeds, it leads*' school of journalism. Harry hit all the right notes in his pitch of the new series. "Indians—Rape—Murder—Fugitive—the Underdog being victimized by Racial Injustice; that was just for openers. "This can all be ours if we move on it now." Then Harry hit the hot button clincher, "Before Hearst gets the scoop."

SOLD! Two hours later, Joe Pulitzer himself approved the deal. He'd not let Billy Hearst beat him to such a bloody good story. Harry Hamlet and Jack Chase would leave tonight and be in Nevada by November 10th. Pulitzer's corporate attorney would find new representation for Samuel Winnemucca while his men were enroute.

Harry left word with Wilson Finch at the Union Cattle Company. "Tell Virgil that Jack and I will see you fellas in three days. Samuel will have the best possible attorney. I don't know who that's going to be yet, but we'll be in touch with a name."

* * *

Pulitzer's corporate attorney, Nicodemus Smith, knew the perfect man for the job. Harley Ainsworth was a master orator who loved the sound of his own voice. He was known as the "Silver-Tongued Sunbeam of the Painted Desert."

Born in a covered wagon in Northern Nevada, Harley had started out as a cowboy on his father's ranch. While working as a jail guard, he studied the law at night. Moving south to Arizona, he'd become a County Prosecutor. When Arizona became a state, Ainsworth went to Congress as one of its two Senators. Currently he was serving as Chairman of the Senate Committee on Indian Affairs.

Nicodemus Smith knew the 6-foot-five-inch tall Ainsworth's reputation for self-promoting. From his broad-brimmed western hat to his Elk's-tooth watch fob, Harley Ainsworth was a showman of the first order.

Smith's plan was to convince Harley that the Winnemucca defense aligned perfectly with his own political interests. Ainsworth only needed to be trial counsel. Elko Attorney Benjamin Parker would handle all the local appearances before the actual trial. Parker would forward to Ainsworth all the information he received in discovery.

Nicodemus Smith was ready to present his choice to Pulitzer. "Joe, if I can talk Harley into putting his name on the case, that alone may garner us a dismissal. Unless the prosecutor has a case tighter than a frog's ass, it will be like Clarence Darrow and William Jennings Bryan are both coming to defend the Indian."

Pulitzer smiled and nodded. "Tell that bag of wind that if he does this for me, my papers will endorse him when he next runs for office, even though he's a Democrat."

Nicodemus Smith immediately called the Senator's office. He explained what needed to happen. Then Smith explained at length how good it would be to have a friend in the newspaper business. Ainsworth signed on with the provision that he could control the timing of the trial and would only have to travel to Elko once.

* * *

Harley Ainsworth put his assistant to work. First, he contacted the Department of Justice for names and points of contact for Nevada's federal judges. Next, he checked with each judge's clerk to find out who had a line into the State Supreme Court. Then the Senator wanted a private phone conference arranged with the Chief Justice of the Nevada Supreme Court.

Judge Angus McGrath sat atop the legal pyramid of the Nevada courts. He remembered Harley Ainsworth from their days as Prosecuting Attorneys in two adjoining counties on different sides of the Nevada state line. "Harley, when are you going to get an honest job and quit your life of crime as a Senator?"

An impromptu retort was in order. "Angus, you old bastard, did you ever learn to write or are you still tracing?" Then after brief shared updates of how the past ten years had treated both men, Ainsworth ran down his wish list of "professional courtesies."

"You know, I'm deeply concerned about Indian issues. I'm going to get back in the legal game by defending one of your Paiutes who's charged with some murders up in Elko County."

"Cut the bullshit, Harley. What do you need?"

"Straight to the point, eh? I always liked that about you, Angus. Anyway, can you arrange for me to be admitted to the Nevada Bar?"

After more reminiscing, McGrath replied that he'd arrange a temporary admission.

"Who's on the criminal bench up there?" McGrath gave Ainsworth both the name of the Elko County judge and a contact for Judge Ronald Wells.

"Angus, thanks a million. If you're ever around these parts and you can scrape the horse shit off your boots, I'll get you a steak dinner at The Willard Hotel. Adios."

* * *

Pulitzer wasted no time in milking the tale he planned to create. Only one day into the story, the *New York World's* headline set the tone.

INJUSTICE IN THE WEST

Four armed men invade a peaceful Indian village to rape and murder a child.

Brave villagers fight back. Authorities charge victim's Father with murder!

Hero Senator to the Rescue!

The article introduced the Cowboy Senator from Arizona touting Ainsworth as the greatest legal mind since Oliver Wendell Holmes and greatest orator since William Jennings Bryan. As chair of the Senate Committee on Indian Affairs, this great man could not let this injustice stand! The 'Silver Tongued Sunbeam of the Painted Desert' was riding to the rescue. Then the article announced their soon-to-begin coverage of the case. *"Don't miss a single installment!"*

Harry Hamlet's editor called his counterpart at a Pulitzer-owned paper in Philadelphia. He arranged for a local reporter to make sure the news of Senator Ainsworth defending Samuel got to Harry Hamlet when the train heading west made a water and coal stop in Philadelphia. Harry would incorporate details about Ainsworth's career and Nevada roots in his next installment.

* * *

"Parker Law Office."

"Senator Harley Ainsworth calling for Benjamin Parker," responded the caller.

"This is Mr. Parker,"

"Please hold for the Senator."

"Mr. Parker, this is Harley Ainsworth. How are you this fine morning?" The Senator didn't wait for the answer to his rhetorical question. He didn't care. "Benjamin, I've heard good things about you already." Ainsworth's first lie.

The unexpected call caught the young attorney totally by surprise. "Thank you, sir," was all he could think to say, not that it would have mattered to Ainsworth, who launched into his monologue.

"I am Chair of the Senate Committee on Indian Affairs." Parker's attempt at polite acknowledgment was submerged in the Senator's verbiage. "Now, I am a native son of the great State of Nevada, born just outside of Winnemucca. When I learned about the injustice, the legal lynching of a fine Paiute Indian, well, that was an inequity I could not allow to stand."

Parker's "Yes, sir," was again lost as Ainsworth thundered on.

"It relieved me to know you were on the case." Another lie.

"While Nevada is far from the capitol it is nonetheless close to my heart and the abiding concerns of my committee."

Ainsworth again missed Parker's next "Yes, sir."

"Would you mind if I was to offer my help in the upcoming trial?" Another rhetorical question and the Senator verbally marched on, not waiting for an answer, as none was wanted.

"Here's what I'd like you to do, litigator to litigator. Send me copies of all the information you collect. Can you do that?" On he marched. "You will be in complete charge all the way through. This is your case to win, son. But I'll be there at the defense table right beside you."

Attorney Parker snuck in a quick, "Thank you."

"I go way back in the legal community out there. Why I was...." Inserting a minor note of self-deprecation, "...but enough about me." Never true.

"I've been in contact with my old friend, Angus McGrath." Keeping to the familiar for emphasis, Senator Ainsworth galvanized his connections to power. "Angus is getting me temporarily admitted to your state bar. He'll also have a word with your local Judge, Ronald Wells, about accommodating my schedule."

Stunned by the call, Parker, breathed a sigh of relief when he heard, "Well, keep up the excellent work," and the phone line clicked to silence. When the attorney finally took the receiver from his ear, he stopped to stare at it for a moment.

What the hell just happened?

18. Pulitzer's Prize Story

Harry Hamlet and Jack Chase began their series during the train trip west. First, Harry recapped for the readers the Jarbidge Robbery, the trial, and the kidnapping of Galli Winnemucca. Then he moved on to the career of Harley Ainsworth. Local Pulitzer stringers collected his columns as the train passed through their towns. Harry passed along instructions and took in recent developments, information or directions the stringers relayed.

Harry and Jack arrived in Elko two days after the arraignment where, as expected, Samuel Winnemucca was charged with four counts of murder. His attorney entered pleas of not guilty on his behalf. A preliminary hearing was calendared for two weeks later.

Harry and Jack checked into the Commercial Hotel. The plan was to use Elko as a base of operations. They'd rent a car and drive to Deeth the next day. That night after dinner at the Basque Hotel, Harry and Jack reviewed the list of interviews they'd developed on the train ride west.

The list would undoubtedly grow after they met with their friends in Deeth and toured what was left of the Paiute encampment and the murder scene. But first, they'd meet the local attorney and visit Samuel with a message that help was on the way.

Attorney Benjamin Parker was awaiting the two at his office. Unlike Harley Ainsworth, the reporter listened more than he talked. Attorney Parker shared what information he'd already collected and his strategy for the impending trial. He gave a brief status report; entry of not guilty pleas and the scheduled Preliminary Hearing in two weeks.

Jack Chase staged photos inside the attorney's office and exterior shots of Parker in front of the county jail and on the courthouse steps. Then the three men went to see Samuel in his jail cell.

Harry and Jack knew what Ben Parker was now learning. The big Indian spoke only when necessary to communicate something of importance. Hamlet expected to do more talking and very little listening.

Sheriff Escuraga was informed of the reporter's pending arrival. His permission had already been given to the jail, so all three men were expected. Secured by two sets of shackles, Samuel smiled when he recognized Harry and Jack. The Indian's jail garb strained to fit his massive shoulders. As Hamlet looked across the table that separated the prisoner from them, Harry tried to identify what he was seeing. *Resolve, resignation? No, he's at peace within himself.*

Harry kept his message brief. "We're here to tell your story and see that you get a fair trial. Mr. Pulitzer is sending an attorney to help Mr. Parker. Sam, you have friends that are doing whatever they can to help. Don't give up hope."

Sam appreciated his friends' efforts to buoy his spirits but he already knew his own fate at the gentle hands of white justice.

* * *

A rented Model T Ford sedan was waiting at the Commercial Hotel the next morning. Harry phoned ahead to the cattle

167

company office and set a meeting for that afternoon at the Deeth Sheriff's office. Familiar faces welcomed Harry and Jack. Virgil and Shorty, Jim Graves and Bill McCabe, and Libby and Verrall Black were all in attendance. Harry would spend more time with each of Samuel's defenders, but for now he needed an overview. Especially, Harry wanted to know why did each pair believed Sam to be innocent?

Harry learned how Phineas Franklin had provoked the town into trying to confiscate guns in the Paiute village. The empty shotgun in the Winnemucca's wickiup made Franklin's claim a lie. His men who were in that home did not take the gun. Instead they took a young girl's life and probably her innocence. Defiling the bodies of Cannon and Edison signified an ultimate shaming by the Paiutes.

Libby Black told how polio had crippled her daughter, Melba, and taken Samuel's wife, Pamahas. Five hundred Paiutes had been dancing, hoping to free their bands from the invisible enemy.

Jim and Bill repeated Samuel's confession, "I killed the four white men who raped and killed my daughter." This was a damning admission from Samuel to the two deputies. Perhaps the loss of his wife and then the rape and murder of Galli had put Samuel temporarily out of his mind?

Harry Hamlet outlined what he needed for his series. He listed what interviews he wanted and which images he needed for Jack's camera. He shared what he knew about the legal experience of Harley Ainsworth, who was receiving updates as information emerged.

"What will the prosecution do next?" asked Harry.

"They need some evidence to corroborate Sam's confession. Did someone see him do the shooting? Do the bullets from the bodies match the rifle he had when they arrested him?" Jim looked at Bill, checking if he had it wrong or was forgetting anything. Bill had nothing to add.

* * *

168

While Harry Hamlet was in his meeting in Deeth, Prosecutor Miles was in conference with Sheriff Escuraga's lone criminalist, Ora Mayer.

"What the hell do you mean the bullets don't match? You're wrong, God damn it. You must be wrong."

The Sheriff stood by. Better to let Miles fume than try to defend a fact that hurt the prosecution.

Mayer sighed. "Here's the deal. We have Winnemucca's rifle. The bullets from the Griswold bodies came from different guns, several guns in fact. There were no slugs recovered from Cannon's body, and the Edison slugs were too deformed for comparison. Sorry." The criminalist returned a blank stare to the red-faced prosecutor, whose future political career was vanishing before his eyes.

Abarran Escuraga had no better answers for Miles. "Donald, why don't we go back to my office and we can talk there?" He held the door open and gestured for Miles that it was truly time to go.

Back in the Sheriff's private office, Miles said, "Abarran, I need your people to find me a witness. Without the ballistics matches, the confession sounds damning but isn't worth a pinch of shit if I can't back it up in some fashion."

"I'll try, Donald. That's all I can promise."

True to his word, Sheriff Escuraga called Jim Graves in Deeth. He told Graves about their failing to match the killing slugs to Winnemucca's gun. "Donald Miles is beside himself with fear about losing the case. He's already staked out a position, 'Defender of civilization from the savage hordes.' Please see about finding a credible witness."

"I'll do what I can. When we went into the encampment with the help of the Elko deputies the Paiutes had pretty much already cleared out. Phil Gray and Arli Cavender were with us. I'll ask if they know anything I missed."

* * *

When the core group of Samuel's supporters next met, Jim Graves shared what he'd just learned from Sheriff Escuraga. There was no ballistics match between Sam's rifle and the bodies.

Harry Hamlet understood the implication. "Jim, can I tell Ben Parker this?"

Graves considered for a full minute before answering. "We'd better not tell Parker yet. He'll find out eventually, but to tell him now would convince my boss he can't trust me to keep my damn mouth shut." The group showed their understanding of Jim's problem.

It was Shorty Roberts who came up with a workable compromise. "Nan nwee snay not to nake any ndeal?" The other seven heads all turned Shorty's way, considering the cowboy's thought. Then every eye turned to Jim Graves and they waited for him to weigh in.

"Harry, correct me if I'm wrong, but here's the way I see it." Seven people leaned forward. "I doubt we'll find any witnesses. Without the bullet match, all Miles has is Sam's confession. He'll keep that problem hidden for as long as he can. He may even finesse his way through the Preliminary Hearing before he has to tell Parker and Ainsworth, but it will come out."

"I agree" said Harry Hamlet. "Miles' only play will be to offer a plea bargain and hope for a conviction without having to go to trial."

Verrall leaned in. "So he's put himself out on a limb by his public statement to the newspapers. If he has to dismiss his own case for lack of evidence, the same papers will saw off the limb behind him."

"I like that," said Jim Graves.

The group agreed that Harry would inform Ben Parker 'just enough' to prevent any consideration of taking a deal, as Shorty Roberts had suggested. It was also agreed that Harry would not use the 'inside information' in any of his pieces; again to protect Jim Graves. The call to Benjamin Parker was made later that morning.

"Ben, this is Harry Hamlet. I have something for you. You can't have all I know, but I'd like to give you what you need for now. If I do this, don't ask me questions or ever name me as a source. Can you live with that?"

"I can. Go ahead."

"Don't make any plea deal with Miles, no matter how good they sound. Understood?"

"Understood." Ben was no fool. He hung up the phone, smiling.

Jim Graves and Bill McCabe spoke to every Indian in the Deeth Paiute band. No one had witnessed Samuel Winnemucca extracting justice from his daughter's killers. Graves informed the sheriff two days later.

That night the deputies were sharing a beer with the newspaper men after they'd toured the encampment site. Jack Chase captured the view from the camp up to Indian Hill and the scorched earth where the murder scene had once been. Virgil and Shorty were also at the table. They heard about Jim's call to his boss and what that did to the prosecution's case.

"Snerves na vastard nright."

Then Virgil added his own bit of cowboy wisdom. "In our business we call that all hat and no cattle."

* * *

Back in the Te-Moak village, Juanita Wewa-Contreras read the looks from her in-laws. *They wonder if I contributed to Samuel's capture.* Out of their sight, she began checking daily with Sheriff Escuraga about when Joaquin could get into the polio ward. The fact that he had not received an admissions date for the boy progressed from worry into a source of panic and rage.

171

Abarran Escuraga was not part of the double cross Wells and Miles had engineered, but now he could not help her. "Juanita, I just don't know. I will ask the Judge. I promise to find you as soon as there is any news."

Her life centered on helping Joaquin to breathe. As his condition grew worse and the promised hospital bed never emerged, Juanita smelled a piscatorial odor. If they had tricked her, there would be hell to pay.

Seventeen days had passed since Samuel's arrest. Prosecutor Miles finessed his way through the preliminary hearing. The confession heard by Deputies Graves and McCabe was sufficient. Harley Ainsworth's assistant and Judge Wells' clerk quietly orchestrated the trial date two months hence.

Publicly, Donald Miles milked the case for all possible attention. Privately, he began trying to strike a plea deal with Parker and Ainsworth. A deal was his only out. There was no corroborating evidence to support the confession, no ballistics and no witnesses. Three times he offered an increasingly better deal. And three times, Attorney Parker rejected the offers. Finally, Donald Miles went back to see Judge Wells.

"Donald, you don't look so well. What did you do?"

Miles told Wells about the continued rejections of his ever-better plea bargains.

The Judge considered. "My best advice is to go over Parker's head, directly to Ainsworth. Make him an offer he can't resist. He wins and can claim that his mere involvement in the case scared you off. You can still claim the win. I know it's not the best, but it's the best you can do. And for Christ sake, do it now."

Donald Miles took the Judge's advice and made contact with Senator Ainsworth's office in Washington. Winnemucca could plead to one count of manslaughter and serve twelve years. Senator Ainsworth could proclaim victory from the court house steps. Donald Miles would say the prosecution was moved by empathy for Winnemucca's

172

deceased wife and murdered daughter. He'd balanced the scales of justice with compassion. Win-win.

Benjamin Parker was never consulted by Harley Ainsworth about the plea deal offer. Knowing Parker was originally picked to be Donald Miles' patsy, Ainsworth's office simply informed him of the new court date and what would happen. His small reward would be to stand beside a legal giant in court and hope that Ainsworth remembered his name.

19. Lynch Mob

Wendell Douglas aspired to rise to the top of the Elko law enforcement community. His current job as a Police Sergeant was only a stepping stone. He'd set his sights on becoming the next Elko County Sheriff. For his wish to come true, he must defeat incumbent Sheriff Abarran Escuraga. Douglas needed something that set him apart in the minds of the public from the soft-spoken Basque. He viewed the upcoming Winnemucca trial as a golden opportunity.

Douglas had one advantage when he announced his candidacy. His father-in-law owned the Elko Daily News. If Douglas could skillfully and discretely discredit Escuraga in the public eye, he was their alternative in the March 1917 election. Unhampered by scruples and with an editorial voice at the newspaper, Douglas made his move. He'd be an instigator, but the public must not know.

The information a free lunch or a free drink could buy was considerable. Everyone likes to talk and relishes setting themselves apart with their "inside information."

Deputy Arli Cavender let spill the first informational arrow for Douglas's campaign quiver. "The Paiutes shit on the bodies."

Half the men at the table in the back of Stockmen's saloon were city police and half were sheriff's deputies. Deputy

Harry Moulton, like Cavender, had been sworn to secrecy months before in Deeth.

"If the public knew what really happened, they would never stand for what the Sheriff is trying to do," said Douglas, injecting more energy and outrage into the revelations.

"Bastards," mumbled one patrolman.

"A God damn bunch of animals" hissed the other city cop at the table. Wendell leaned back, observing the progress of the fire he'd just started. *Now if I can turn that anger against Abarran, I've got something. I'll tell my Father-in-law and that should get the ball rolling.*

The Editorial page placement was perfect. Best of all, Wendell Douglas had instigated while never publicly agitating.

"PAIUTE PERIL—FOUR KILLED AND BODIES DEFILED!

Nevada has not had a lynching since 1905, but here in the Elko County jail sits a self-confessed murderer. Does the totality of this crime in its violence and depravity make your blood boil? It does mine. Fellow citizens, this crime makes me think fondly of the message sent by 'Old-Time Frontier Justice!' When did we decide that the government knows better than the citizenry how to punish the guilty and protect our own?"

The fuse was lit. Among those having a drink at Stockmen's or any of the other saloons, the tones were angry. As the night dragged on and the liquor flowed freely, the violence in the conversation increased.

Josh Hawley was the first to step forward. The rope he carried advertised his intentions. "I'm going to the jail," was all he had to say. Forty citizens fell in behind Hawley as he headed towards the county cells four blocks away. As a light snow fell, the mob moved quietly through the darkness. Wendell Douglas, the instigator, now hedged his bet. From inside his office at the police station, he called Abarran Escuraga at home.

"Abarran, this is Wendell Douglas. A mob of drunks just went past, and I think they're headed for the jail with a rope. I know you've got only a jailer and one deputy on duty, and I'm here by myself right now. You'd better get down to your jail. I'll monitor the bunch."

Sheriff Escuraga made it to the jail in five minutes and entered through a rear door. The sole night duty deputy, Bradley Cluff, looked up at the sound of the door closing.

"Sheriff, is everything all right?"

The sheriff spoke as he moved to the door of the department's small armory. "Brad, grab a shogun and come with me. You are to lock the door behind me and then get upstairs to the cells. You and the jailer lock the door to the cell block and post up outside Winnemucca's cell. No one comes in."

Sheriff Escuraga, shotgun in hand, walked down the hall and out the building's front doors. Deputy Cluff did as ordered, locking the doors behind his boss, who now stood alone in the falling snow.

The mob turned the final corner and moved toward the jail where Abarran Escuraga waited. The only sound was the rhythmic crunch of their boots on the snow-crusted street.

Joshua Hawley raised his arm, simultaneously stopping his group and showing Escuraga the rope. "Sheriff, we want Winnemucca. Stand aside and let the will of the people be done."

Sheriff Escuraga stood his ground.

"You are all alone, Sheriff."

With his shotgun held at port arms, Abarran Escuraga looked out over the mob, trying to recognize familiar faces before he spoke. "Joshua—Randolph—Lee, I know many of you and this nonsense needs to stop. Go home now."

"Step aside" and Hawley lowered his arm and stepped to the bottom of the jail house stairs, confident the mob would follow.

"Fellas, they say that the loudest sound in the world is the slamming of a cell door." Escuraga paused, still searching the forty faces. "Actually, that's not true. The loudest sound in the world is this. Listen." He pumped a 12 gauge, .00 buck shot shell into the shotgun, 'ka-chunk—ka chunk.'

Again Escuraga paused. "That is the loudest sound you'll ever hear, and for some of you it may also be the last sound you ever hear."

"You're all alone, sheriff," said Hawley, his volume rising.

"Well, there is only one mob, so I don't need any help. Last chance, fellas." and the shotgun barrel lowered so Joshua Hawley could glimpse his own future in the black quarter-size muzzle.

When Hawley turned to his followers, he only saw backs fast melting away into the silence of the falling snow. Alone now, the leader became the follower as he, too, slunk away into the night. Sheriff Escuraga lowered the muzzle of his shotgun and turned to reenter his office through the back door. *Stupid borrachos.*

20. The Trial

The job of breaking the bad news to Juanita fell to Sheriff Escuraga. There was no hospital bed for Joaquin. Since Abarran's family had tended sheep on some of Juanita's Father's Double-Diamond ranch land, she might accept the bad news best from him.

"Lo siento, Juanita, I'm so sorry, but the hospital has no room for Joaquin. I don't know how hard they tried, but it is what Mr. Miles and Judge Wells tell me."

"The Judge and Mr. Miles both promised me!" Juanita began to sob quietly. Abarran stared at the floor. He had not been a part of the lie they had sold her, but that was cold comfort now as he stood beside the weeping mother.

Two days before Samuel Winnemucca's court date, Senator Harley Ainsworth arrived in Elko. His entourage included an executive assistant, a secretary and a U.S. Marshal acting as a bodyguard. That night was a quiet evening with a hosted dinner at the home of Newton

Crumley. The next day, Ainsworth would meet his client and co-counsel for the first time.

Benjamin Parker arrived at his new partner's hotel room at 9:00 A.M. with Harry Hamlet at his side. The bodyguard opened the suite door and the two were ushered in.

Harley Ainsworth, a dressing gown still covering his suit trousers, shirt, and vest. stood. "Mr. Parker, I presume," Ainsworth said to Harry Hamlet.

Harry used his index finger to gesture towards the diminutive Parker. "I'm Harry Hamlet, the Pulitzer reporter. This is Mr. Parker."

"Well, it is indeed a pleasure to meet you both. Mr. Hamlet, I have to admit it is an unexpected pleasure in your case. As you well know, I have always been a defender—an ardent defender—of our free press. Mr. Parker and I have some important legal strategy to discuss, so if you'd excuse us..."

But for the first time, Benjamin Parker, designated patsy, interrupted the Senator.

"Sir, you need to hear what Harry has to say. It may well change your legal strategy for tomorrow. Please."

Whether entertained by the impertinent upstart attorney or just curious, Ainsworth motioned to chairs and the three men sat.

"Senator, we think the prosecutor has no case and we'd like you to reject the plea agreement. Move for a dismissal," said Parker.

Ainsworth nodded with the indulgent condescension of a parent to a child. "And why do you think so, counselor?"

Now Harry Hamlet took the lead. "Senator, what I do is investigate and collect facts. Here are the facts that are being hidden from you. The prosecution's entire case is based on the confession. There is no ballistics match, no witnesses to the shooting and no other evidence." Harry now leaned back in his seat as Ainsworth stopped smiling.

His tone one of skepticism, Ainsworth spoke. "And why are we only hearing this now?"

With newfound courage, Ben Parker jumped in. "Because once his deal was in place, the legal requirement of disclosure was conveniently bypassed. The plea offer was Donald Miles's self-serving way to salvage a win from a losing case. His political future is so far in the weeds that the rabbits are going to get him."

Now it was Ainsworth's turn. Sitting back in his seat he asked, "Are you absolutely sure about what the prosecution does not have? I mean dead sure?" His cold eyes concealed his skepticism that a legal unknown could be presenting such a made-to-order winning strategy. If it was true, Ainsworth was being handed a legal gold nugget.

Both Hamlet and Parker answered without hesitation. "Yes, we are. Don't take the deal."

Ainsworth sat in silence, considering how to make the best use of the additional information. Finally, an answer emerged. "I'll take you both at your word. I know how to play this. Now what say you introduce me to my client?

* * *

"Lo siento, mi hijo, I'm so sorry." said Juanita as she held the pillow down on Joaquin's face. Already being suffocated by polio, the child may not have noticed his mother helping him to the other side.

She then checked the pistol in her purse and began her walk to Elko. As she walked, Juanita thought about the list of mortal sins she was accruing. She had committed murder and the worst of all possible mortal sins, despairing of God's forgiveness and of her son's recovery. She would be in the courtroom to commit another sin when court convened at 10:00 A.M.

Yesterday on the jail steps, Senator Ainsworth had expounded on his deep and abiding concern for Nevada, the place of his birth, and for the Indians who inhabited the country. With flowing rhetoric Ainsworth spread forth the depth and breadth of his legal acumen for all to view.

Today the self-proclaimed legal titan stood in an Elko County courtroom defending an Indian from being victimized by a heartless system. Ainsworth would use every trick he knew to bathe himself in the light of a legal savant, and expose Prosecutor Donald Miles as a heartless, racist scoundrel.

Senator Ainsworth's bodyguard sat in the very last row of the courtroom. Juanita Wewa-Contreras took an aisle seat in the first row behind Donald Miles. Harry Hamlet and Jack Chase sat in the first row behind the defense table, with Sam's six other defenders fanned out behind them.

Harley Ainsworth, Benjamin Parker and their client were at the defense table. Donald Miles was alone at the Prosecution table. Samuel Winnemucca was still double shackled and two armed deputies stood quietly along the walls opposite both sets of attorneys.

With all parties in their places, the Bailiff gave two sharp raps on the door to the judge's chambers and the Honorable Ronald Wells took the bench. All in attendance stood as the judge entered. The three attorneys and the defendant briefly stood when the Court Clerk called the case. The familiar steps of the courtroom waltz began with the first directions from its conductor, Judge Wells.

"Good morning everyone, Mr. Miles, I understand that you have reached a plea agreement with the defense?" Prosecutor Miles rose from his table and spun into his first graceful pirouette.

"I have, your honor. Defendant Winnemucca will plead guilty to one count of manslaughter and serve a sentence of twelve years." Miles' eyes remained on the Judge, while Wells' focus turned to the defense table.

"Senator Ainsworth, it is an honor to have the most famous native son of Humboldt County in my court."

Both attorneys and the defendant stood. Since Judge Wells had ignored Benjamin Parker's presence at the table, Harley Ainsworth now moved to correct the oversight. The larger Ainsworth half-turned to his left and placed an enormous hand on his colleague's shoulder.

"Thank you Judge. It is my honor to assist Elko's own Benjamin Parker in Mr. Winnemucca's defense. I am a mere assistant."

To avoid an unseemly break in courtroom decorum, Ronald Wells acknowledged the other attorney. "Yes, of course, Mr. Parker. Now down to business. Is the defendant ready to enter his plea?" Ben Parker turned to his co-counsel Harley Ainsworth, who stood waiting, his verbal knife in hand. The graceful dance was about to become an assassination.

"If the court will indulge me for just a moment." Ainsworth made a self-effacing pause before continuing. "From our far distant national capitol, I have somehow missed the prosecution's response to our Mr. Parker's discovery motion." Ainsworth waited two beats and then flashed the knife to Miles.

"I apologize to the court and opposing counsel; it has been too long since I've been engaged in the practice of law. I have to ask, is it still the case that a confession must be supported by some bit of evidence in order to be valid?" Ainsworth sank his verbal blade into the prosecutor's heart.

All three attorneys, deputies, Bailiff, and local and national press silently waited for Judge Wells to make a pronouncement from the bench. The look of surprise in the Judge's eyes changed into one of concern. Ronald Wells was about to twist Ainsworth's knife. *I hope that jackass doesn't piss back on me. I can deny anything he says.* The courtroom silence broke when Judge Wells spoke.

"Yes, that is still the case Mr. Ainsworth." Wells paused. "Mr. Miles?"

The name hung over the prosecution's table. All eyes switched from the judge to the prosecutor. The only sound

182

Donald Miles recognized was the loud pounding of his own heart.

"Mr. Miles," repeated Wells.

There was no escape. Miles only faint hope was to soften his landing from the fall he saw just ahead. "Your honor, I apologize to the defense. In light of the defendant's confession to two deputy sheriffs, I did not see the need to pursue other evidence." Miles' lie only dug the hole deeper. Ainsworth pounced.

"I appreciate the Court's indulgence. Is Mr. Miles saying he has neither ballistics evidence matching the murder weapon nor a witness to the crime?"

Gasps were heard from somewhere in the courtroom gallery. Comfortable with his own plausible deniability, Judge Wells allowed Donald Miles to remove the last two shovels of dirt from his legal grave.

Red faced and sweating, Prosecutor Miles choked out, "No we do not."

A few curses were audible over a universal background titter that filled the courtroom.

Mercifully, neither Parker nor Ainsworth jumped on his final half-truth. Harley nudged the younger lawyer. It was time to dispatch their victim. Harley Ainsworth would take his own victory lap on the court house steps.

Ben Parker rose. "Your honor, in light of the prosecution's failure to establish any case against my client, I ask the court to dismiss all charges against Mr. Winnemucca."

Judge Wells didn't pause for an instant. "Motion granted. Mr. Winnemucca is released from custody."

The audience broke into cheers and animated congratulations. Harry Hamlet and his friends were all leaning over the half-wall that separated the court area from the audience. Deputy Phil Gray switched from guarding his prisoner to removing his shackles.

Juanita sat through the proceedings. Her only thoughts were of her own damnation for what she had already done and was about to do. *So many mortal sins.*

Juanita passed unnoticed through the swinging gate and stopped behind the seated figure of Donald Miles. She whispered in his ear, "*Gusano*, such a worm," just before she pulled the trigger and decorated the table with his brains. The sound of the shot cut through the noise and commotion of the courtroom scene and froze everyone in place. Juanita approached the bench, pistol in hand. She was two steps past the prosecution table when Judge Wells noticed her approach and her gun.

His one moment of hesitation as he recognized the threat was too long. Juanita's second shot caught him squarely in the chest and down Wells dropped. The Bailiff and the other extra deputy now faced her, their guns drawn.

Juanita Wewa-Contreras turned and locked eyes with Samuel Winnemucca, her face in a thin, sad smile. "You were the only honest, honorable man. You lied to protect your people. I lied to myself by believing I could trade your life for my son's. Lo siento, Samuel," and she fired her last shot into her own brain.

The End

184

Acknowledgements

After writing Spirit Lake Payback, I was searching for inspiration and had pretty much decided to connect the 1916 polio epidemic to what's happening in 2020 with Covid-19. Educating myself about polio I read, *POLIO: An American Story*, by David Oshinsky, and, *In the Shadow of POLIO*, by Kathryn Black. Continuing my own background education I happened on the fact that New York City had the highest infection rate in the nation. But when I looked at infection by states, Nevada had the worst rate.

Then I was moved by a source closer to home and heart. Before her passing, my mother, Doris Black Scott, penned, *Reflections of my Childhood in Deeth, Nevada*. Her memories included the Paiute Indians and their gathering at Indian Hill. Also, how the family encountered a local man on the road to Elko and helped him evade an armed searcher. Finally, how her Father grubstaked a miner who discovered gold in Jarbidge Canyon. That led me to the last U. S. Mail wagon robbery in the country.

My paternal grandfather, Francis Scott, was a commercial photographer in Elko. His daughter, my Aunt Vivian, spent the majority of her life on crutches, having contracted the disease while working as a nurse.

I also heard about polio victims who were known to my maternal grandmother, Sarah Black. I, myself, was one of the first graders who was lined up in a school parking lot in 1955 for my first dose of the Salk polio vaccine.

Now my research switched to learning about the Paiute Indians through *Life Among the Paiutes* by Sara Winnemucca. In her work, I learned about how the Ghost Dance of the Plains Indians had Paiute origins.

My work of fiction is an attempt to combine significant true events with my own recollections of multiple visits to Deeth, Starr Valley, Lamoille Canyon and Elko, Nevada.

Last but not least I owe a continuing debt to my courageous volunteer readers and consultants: Dr. Jay

Hunter, M.D.; David Quinn; Glen Lanier; Louise Regelin; Gary and Beverly Fuller; Lynne Whisner; Amy Johnston; Monica Ray; Monique Lillard; and Dave Gressard. I would also be lost without Gordon Long, my editor. They all struggle mightily to save me from my own literary mistakes. My friend, artist Mike McCoy, was also a volunteer reader and contributed artwork.

About the Author

After returning from the Air Force, Stu Scott worked as staff in a juvenile detention facility, moving on to adult probation and finally to federal probation and parole. Simultaneously, in 1980 he returned to the military as a reserve agent with the Army Criminal Investigation Command. Born and raised in the San Francisco bay area, he has lived with his wife in Moscow, Idaho since 1981. Believing that we only go around once in life and that one job is never enough, his other careers include: professional winemaker, college instructor, director of a school for disabled children and as a stained glass artist. His introduction to commercial writing came as an outgrowth of an introduction to the therapeutic value of 'journaling' as part of a Veterans' PTSD counseling group.

SLS@Turbonet.com

Also By This Author

The Tooth Fairy

A story as cold as a Spokane winter about what happens
when a crook chooses the wrong victim.

The Grand Tetons

The Texas bank robber who carries twin 38's.

Idaho Catch and Release

Husband and wife pornographers who give a new meaning
to what's really a crime.

The Deal

The 1976 case of a crooked politician revisited in 2016.

Available at Amazon in paperback and on Kindle

ISBN:9781732246812

The Grand Tetons

It was a hot August day in 1969 when Janet Lee walked into the center of Clarksville, Texas from where she parked her car in the Seven Eleven lot by the highway. Her home town in Oklahoma looked just like this one. The square of every small Texas town had either a courthouse or a city hall on one side. Across the square was the bank, and between the two, in the center of the square, was a flagpole with a cannon at its base. The red, white and blue of the Texas flag hung just below Old Glory. With no breeze, the two flags blended into one mass of colors.

"I wonder if this is the Clarksville that The Monkees sang about?" she muttered as she crossed the square. The Walmart that had come to town last year had already driven out many of the local merchants. The storefronts on the square were all empty except for the Farmers and Merchants Bank. That was all she needed. It was more than that. It was a gift, and you could make more of it.

Entering the bank, Janet let her eyes adjust to the interior lighting. A manager sat at a desk in the rear of the lobby. She doodled on a withdrawal slip before taking it over to the lone teller who stood at one of the three stations.

"Hello." She switched on her most dazzling smile, tossed her ash-blond hair and beamed at the young man with her bright blue eyes.

"Good morning Ma'am." He flushed. "Ar...eh...I mean good afternoon." He finally managed to get out, "How can I help you today?"

"Well thank you." She smiled and passed the withdrawal slip across the counter. "I'd like to make a withdrawal, please."

Slowly she opened the front of her short denim jacket, first one side and then the other, to reveal the white fishnet of her tank top. The smile on the face of the young man disappeared. His eyes were drawn to the rose-pink nipples that seemed to be staring at him through the mesh. He tried looking back up to her brilliant smile but couldn't. From her round, firm breasts the rosy nipples were still staring up at his eyes. Then his gaze dropped to the large brown wood gun butt that hugged the flat of her stomach. Some emblem, a Texas star perhaps, was inset on the grip.

"Take all the money from your drawer and put it in the bag, honey." She held eye contact with him, even though his stare had not yet left the gun. She removed a white flour sack from her back pocket and passed it across the counter. "Please don't spoil either of our days by pushing any alarm. Momma needs the money for her surgery, and I'm just trying to be a good daughter."

When the full bag slid back across the counter, she spoke again. "Wait just a bit before you do anything." She did her best to portray both innocence and vulnerability by managing a small frown. Then, buttoning the middle button on her jacket, she walked out of the bank, but not out of his dreams.

* * *

"So can you tell me what she was wearing?" asked Deputy Sheriff Muldrow, from Red River County.

"Denim jeans and a denim jacket," was the response. The answer from the teller started the deputy writing in his notebook as they sat across the table in the bank's employee lounge.

"What color was her hair?"

"I don't remember." The teller stared at the table, avoiding eye contact with the deputy.

"What about the color of her eyes?"

"I don't remember." The deputy pressed on.

"Did she have a gun?"

"Yes, there was a gun."

At last they we're back on track. "Okay, what kind of a gun was it?"

"Big gun." He shook his head apologetically.

Trying not to let his frustration show, the deputy tried again. "Is there anything else you can recall?" The teller didn't seem to hear the question. After what seemed like a minute, Muldrow repeated the question.

"She had a beautiful smile. I just couldn't seem to tear my eyes away."

"From her smile?"

"Yes that's right, from her smile." Then he shut up. He wasn't about to volunteer that all he could recall were her beautiful breasts.

* * *

Janet Lee Durham sat in her yard swing back home in Idabel, Oklahoma, and counted the money from the Clarksville bank: $1,562. Checking that no one was around, she tucked the bills into her tank top and went back into the house. Fishing the loot out from her cleavage, she added it to the dollars already in a bag balm tin hidden in the bottom of her underwear drawer.

Janet Lee was the only daughter of Ray and Thelma Mahoney and had grown up in Idabel. She'd learned to fight from her three brothers, but she'd learned to drink bourbon—with a beer back—from her father. She'd learned how to handle a gun in the military police.

Most important to her recent success was what she had learned about men. It had been a long tutorial that started in the back seat of a Pontiac convertible during high school. Men who found her irresistible were easily led. They would follow her anywhere if, either literally or figuratively, she had ahold of their dicks.

Better still, all she really had to do was make men want her. Beyond being smart, confident and beautiful, Janet Lee Durham was tough. She was well armed with the big Colt revolver her father had given her when she graduated from the Military Police School at Fort McClelland, Alabama, and just as lethal...with her irresistible sex appeal.

* * *

De Kalb, Texas, was in Bowie County, 25 miles east of Clarksville. Janet Lee figured that the sheriffs in the two adjacent counties wouldn't be expecting another robbery so soon after the Clarksville job.

Three days after Clarksville, Janet Lee pulled into DeKalb. She passed the Walmart on the way in and parked one block off the town square. The scene was only different because this county courthouse was built out of red sandstone instead of brick. The one-time bank building was now home to the Red River Army Depot Credit Union. Crossing the street past the obligatory cannon, she stopped to look down the muzzle. An empty Dr. Pepper can peered back with its cyclops-like pop-top eye.

"Well, you are real at least." She gave the cannon barrel a pat. "I was wondering if they got a bulk price on you guys from Cannons 'R' Us." From the cannon, Janet Lee had a clear view inside the credit union, right through its large, plate-glass windows. The lobby was empty like the storefronts that ringed the square.

Today she had dressed in tight brown slacks, a matching waist-length jacket, boots and a white cowboy hat. She wore large gold hoop earrings. Looking good and feeling better, she strode into the lobby of the credit union. Stopping to pretend to write out a deposit slip gave her a moment to study the lobby and decide if there was a suitable teller she could target. There was.

"Hello, may I help you?" The middle-aged teller's hair was receding at the temples, with gray starting to appear. Janet Lee smiled back as she slowly opened her jacket. His glasses slid down his nose as he lowered his gaze to her chest. Her breasts strained the mesh of her fishnet top, one nipple peeking proudly out while the other strained enticingly against the mesh. She detected the brief move of his eyes from her chest to the gun butt showing above her silver and gold belt buckle.

"You're cute, mister," Janet Lee said with a smile. "Please don't spoil this day for either of us. I'll be gone in one minute, and I need the money for my tuition. Please put the cash from your drawer right into this bag," and she passed the same flour sack to him.

He emptied the contents of his drawer into her bag and passed it back. She also removed one of his business cards from the card rack on the counter.

"John Stevens, it's been a pleasure doing business with you. Please keep this transaction our little secret for, say... five minutes. If you do that for me, I won't come calling at your house." She waved his card in her fingers. Buttoning the middle button of her jacket, she turned and left. John Stevens silently watched her go. When fully out of his trance, he walked briskly from the teller cages to the desk of his manager.

"Mr. Majeski, I just got robbed."

* * *

The day after the robbery, John was seated at the table in the staff break room, a glass of water in his hand, when the manager came in with the one and only DeKalb City Police detective.

"John, I'm Detective Lambert. Getting robbed is pretty upsetting isn't it?" John didn't look up from his water glass,

193

but nodded in agreement. Lambert took a seat across the table.

"I'd like you to tell me what you can about the robbery. What did the robber look like? What was said? Was there a note presented? Did you see a gun? Just tell me what you can,"

"I'll leave you two alone," said the branch manager and left the room. Stevens and Lambert sat silently for several minutes.

Finally, the detective broke the silence. "Listen, you didn't do anything wrong, here. Nobody is unhappy with you. The money is insured and no one got hurt; that's what counts. How about you begin with when you first saw the robber. Just start talking and we'll sort out what I need."

"She was young and very blond. Nicely dressed in a western-cut suit... and she wore a white Stetson."

"What color were her eyes?"

"I didn't notice." This was a lie that couldn't be challenged.

"Can you guess her height or weight? Was her build slim, medium, or heavy?"

"Honestly, once I saw her," and John paused—a long pause—before continuing. "When I saw her gun...after that I didn't pay too much attention to what she looked like. All I could see was her..." He paused again, swallowing, "...gun."

"That's okay John; guns are pretty unnerving. Did she point it at you?"

"Ah no, she just opened her jacket and showed me what she had." It would be safer to lie by omission. He preferred emphasizing the rise in his blood pressure caused by Janet's opening her jacket, and didn't mention the rise in his pants.

"Anything else you can remember? How about the gun? Was it a revolver or an automatic? Was it black or nickel?"

"Sorry, all that I can say is that what I saw looked big. I'll never forget what I saw if I live to be a hundred. I relive that image whenever I close my eyes."

194

Janet Lee Durham had only one heart's desire when she began robbing banks. She wanted to trade off her shit-box Ford pickup and get the 'Judge' model, 1969 Pontiac GTO. What girl wouldn't be seduced by the orange car featured in the Pontiac ad campaign? She longed to feel the leather bucket seats caressing her back. She could imagine the vibrating power of those 389 cubic inches rushing up through her feet to her thighs. After two bank jobs she was half way to the $6,759 she needed for the car.

Janet Lee worked a day job as a waitress in the restaurant her husband managed. Her earning and tips, along with the robbery money—which she had failed to mention to her husband, Jimmy—were all being saved for the car.

"Please God, just this one little thing, and I'll retire from crime and never sin again." Not wanting to lie to God, she quickly amended her prayer. "Well, at least I'll retire from crime." She didn't know if one could pray for God's help in committing a felony, but there seemed to be no harm in asking. It was kind of like dating, she figured; if you never asked, you never got a "yes."

"Baby, that GTO will be the most fun we can have with our clothes on," she told Jimmy when he asked about how her car funding was coming along.

* * *

George Oostergard was the lone FBI agent stationed in Texarkana, Texas. His office was in the federal courthouse at the east end of State Line Boulevard, straddling the Texas and Arkansas border. This allowed the Eastern District of Texas and the Western District of Arkansas to share courtroom space in the same building.

Once a month he attended a Tri-County Investigators meeting. Police and sheriff's detectives from Red River and Bowie counties met with their counterparts from Miller County, Arkansas. Each agency shared details about their ongoing investigations and recent crimes. The meeting usually lasted an hour before the group adjourned for an executive session at Fat Jack's bar.

The Clarksville and DeKalb robberies had both happened within the past ten days. The FBI had jurisdiction over crimes involving federally insured banks and credit unions if the locals chose not to pursue matters under their own state laws. George had not been invited in on either case, perhaps because of the thinly veiled local suspicion of all things federal. The 1865 surrender at Appomattox had ended the fighting but not the distrust between the North and South. Beer or bourbon consumed face to face with colleagues was all they had to break through the institutional suspicions.

Deputy Rick Muldrow from the Red River County Sheriff's Department was having a drink with Detective Skip Lambert from DeKalb PD. Seeing George enter the bar, Muldrow motioned for the FBI Agent to join them.

"George, why is it that you take lots of notes at our meeting, but when it's your turn to speak, you never say shit? Not a damn word." Muldrow's delivered the comment as a friendly ribbing. For the FBI, sharing information was a one-way street.

George could only shake his head. "Fellas, I'm just trying to learn from the real pros. Besides, you know you'd never listen to whatever I had to say anyway. Now which one of you assholes—I mean gentlemen—is going to buy me a beer?"

It was during the second beer that Skip Lambert heard a surprising similarity between his victim at the DeKalb credit union robbery and Rick Muldrow's reluctant bank teller in Clarksville. Skip shared his skepticism about the perception or memory lapses of his victim.

George's curiosity was piqued.

"Would you mind if I had a chat with your victims?" He steepled his fingers. "It does sound like they didn't give up the full story. I wonder why? If I find out anything more, it's yours to use." Oostergard nodded at one then the other of his companions. "At the very least, I can issue and circulate a Crime Alert Bulletin in East Texas and Western Arkansas to all of our officers and the local departments."

"Knock yourself out, George." Detective Lambert leaned back from their table.

"Rick?" Agent Oostergard waited.

"Sure," Muldrow nodded.

* * *

Agent Oostergard arranged for meetings with the two tellers. Each interview took place at the office of the local lead investigator. Lambert and Muldrow observed from out of sight as George interviewed the tellers. He chose to interview Terry Grunsberg, the 21-year-old from Clarksville first. His answers had been the most suspicious, and being younger, he should be easier to break in an interview.

"Terry thanks for coming in today. I'm FBI Special Agent George Oostergard. I'm interested in the robbery because bank robbery is a federal crime. So let me start by going over Deputy Muldrow's notes from his interview. Tell me if anything got left out," and Oostergard read back the interview portion of the crime report provided by the deputy.

"Did we miss anything?

The teller stopped, sipped from a Dr. Pepper and signaled with a shake of his head that nothing had been missed.

"Terry, I've been an agent for more than twenty years. I've got to say that your statement—well son, it didn't pass my personal stink test. So you and I are going to start over with a clean sheet. Now, this is important. I want you to think back to the robbery." Adding emphasis, George slowed his speech and hit on each of the next five words separately. "Give me every little detail."

"Here's the thing; this is now a federal crime. You seem to be a fine young man. I'm sure that your folks are real proud of you. You're making a good start in the working world there at the bank. So I don't want to find out that the reason you're holding back information is because you knew the robber or were in on the plan somehow. That would derail all the good things you've got going. Now, let's get started."

Terry feared pissing off the FBI more than he feared embarrassment. He spilled the whole story about the hot lady bank robber. The teller was now able to describe, in— minute detail—the bank robber's wardrobe, hair color and skin tone. It appeared that once he started talking, he couldn't stop, even venturing so far as to offer a guess about her cup size.

Armed with this new information, Agent Oostergard re-interviewed John Stevens, using the same set-up scenario that had successfully motivated Grunsberg. Then the agent revealed his hole-card.

"I understand that besides looking like every man's wet-dream of a rodeo queen, she made a point of showing you her great knockers. 34-DD's would you say?"

Stevens sighed and they began. An hour later, every detail had been revealed. John clung to his claim that he'd withheld the details because he'd been threatened.

Acting upon what now appeared to be a distinctive crime signature and with more complete information, the bureau sent a Crime Alert Bulletin to all local and federal law enforcement offices in Arkansas, Oklahoma and Texas. At this point, the prosecuting attorneys for the two Texas counties were only too happy to turn over their cases to the federal government. Soon after, a federal grand jury returned a two-count indictment against a Jane Doe. Janet Lee Durham was now a wanted federal fugitive. Fortunately for the feds, she didn't know about the Crime Bulletin when she hit the bank in Paris, Texas.

* * *

The Cattleman's Bank and Trust had the FBI Crime Alert flyer posted in its break room. Since surveillance camera technology had not yet arrived on the bank security scene, the flyer had only a composite sketch of the robber. When Janet showed what was under her coat this time, the young man immediately hit a silent alarm. He then turned and asked the head teller, Mrs. Dorothy Jones, to help him at the window. Dorothy took one look at the young robber and smiled.

"Oh honey, you can put those away. You probably have about another ninety seconds before the cops arrive. I'd be going if I were you."

Janet got only as far as the front door before the first police car arrived. She didn't resist the two officers with drawn guns. When she raised her hands as instructed, all of her weapons were revealed. Sitting behind the cage in the back of the police car, now unarmed, she heard one of the officers in the front seat whistle and say, "Nice tits."

"Yes they are. Eat your heart out."

Looking out through the bars of the patrol car, she glimpsed a GTO, its sleek body gleaming orange, its windows winking in the sunlight. She heard the motor purr and watched as her orange wet dream vanished.

The End

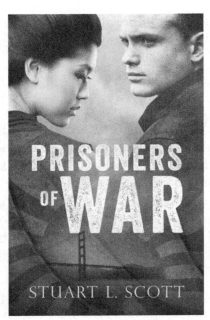

Prisoners of War is simultaneously a love story, a mystery and a history, all woven together. Everything of a historical nature is true to the best of my knowledge and research. Conflict between love and duty. Conflict between love of country and the love of your life. How far would you go to win back your love, when the government has taken her away? Fear, racism and abiding love collide in 1942 America, when your only crime was being born Japanese.

Available at Amazon in paperback and on Kindle

ISBN: 978-1-7322468-2-9

Sample from *Prisoners of War*

Chapter 1: Keyport, 1941

It was late the morning of December 7 when I heard a commotion at the Olson house next door—crying and swearing. It sounded like a family fight, loud and vulgar even, yet personal. Sounds of confusion were also coming from the main gate at the nearby Keyport, Washington, Torpedo Station. I was used to the noise in the Keyport machine shop where I worked, building torpedoes for the Bureau of Ordinance. This was a different sound. Trucks were moving, people were shouting and booted feet were running. Behind me, through his closed door, I heard my roommate Duano's voice.

"God damn it, you guys!"

He emerged half-dressed with jeans and socks on, his shirt and shoes in hand.

"Sunday morning is supposed to be quiet, Pat. What is the problem with those assholes?"

"Come on. Get dressed, and we'll head over to the gate and see what's up."

We walked out past our neighbor's store and into the street. Up ahead, one of the many Marines standing around turned briefly to respond to our shouted question.

"What the hell's going on?"

"The Japs bombed our fleet at Pearl Harbor. We're at war."

His words stopped us both in our tracks. In the confusion at the main gate, I saw a familiar figure, Captain Olson, my landlord and chief of security at Keyport.

"Captain Olson! Is there something we should do to help? Just tell us what you need."

"Thanks, McBride. For now, it would be best for you just to go home until your next shift. If I need to organize work or defense parties, I'll send someone over to get you. Bad business, this."

Then Olson turned away to direct the makeshift barricade being erected outside the gate. Still stunned, Duano and I walked back to our house and sat down on the porch to watch the action at the main gate. I stepped inside and turned on the radio, hoping for, all the while dreading, more news.

The news was on every station. The few details available were being repeated and occasionally augmented when more information came in from across the Pacific. We didn't have a phone, so I tried calling home using the pay phone at the Keyport Mercantile. Again and again I turned the rotary dial, trying to call San Bruno. I tried my parents' house first and then my fiancée's home, but every attempt rang as a busy signal.

Walking away from the pay phone through the bright sun of this particular Sunday morning, I would never have believed that inside of two years I would become a traitor to my country.

* * *

On Monday every worker on shift arrived early, and a somber silence prevailed throughout the building. Each man was greeted upon arrival by his supervisor.

"There will be an announcement over the P.A. at 8 A.M., so don't bother to start work yet."

We understood and shared the mix of pain, outrage and fear that surrounded us all. Moving inside, we gathered in small knots—talking, many smoking—while we waited. Some of the men sat on the row of benches that ran down the center of each aisle of the locker room. I chose to go into the cavernous work room, preferring the cold morning light and familiar comfort of my own work station. Leaning on my workbench as I waited for the announcement, I was soon joined by Andy, who worked at the bench next to me. He nodded but didn't speak.

At precisely 8 A.M. a click came from the speakers mounted near the ceiling. Some of us turned to face the sound; others just looked up or stared off into space. Some never raised their eyes from the shiny, gray cement floor.

"Good morning. This is Commander Munson." His voice was steady and devoid of emotion, with an even pace that faltered only when he listed the casualties. "I have been

202

instructed to read and then post the following cable from the War Department in Washington, D.C.

"Yesterday at just past 8 A.M. local time, naval forces of Japan conducted a surprise attack on elements of our Pacific Fleet at anchor in Pearl Harbor, Hawaiian Islands. Attacking in three waves, Japanese aircraft sunk or severely damaged eight battleships, three cruisers and three destroyers. Loss of aircraft by Marine and Army air-corps units at Hickam Field totaled two hundred sixty-two aircraft. Casualty figures are currently at two thousand killed or wounded with the final total expected to go higher. At 11:06 local time, President Franklin D. Roosevelt addressed Congress and, with only one dissent, Congress voted to declare war on Japan and empowered the president to wage war against Japan with all of the resources of the United States."

I could hear sobbing and cursing in the background. Some of the words were spit out clearly, others more swallowed by the speakers.

"Sons-a-bitches," cursed a faceless voice from the crowd.

Commander Munson spoke again after about 30 seconds of silence, though it seemed more like 30 minutes. "Gentlemen, you are a part of the 'full resources of the United States' that Congress and the president will now use to punish Japan for this cowardly attack. Much will be demanded of us all in the coming days, but I don't expect it to be more than what we can willingly give.

"You will be getting more information from your section leaders in a few moments. God bless you all and God bless the United States."

The P.A. speakers went silent. To a man, none of us moved. In that moment of our shared national outrage, I hated the Japanese as much as any man on the station. My hate for the Japanese arose from their attack on Pearl Harbor and its potential impact on my future. I feared the attack had sunk not only our ships, but also my plans. I worried that Bea, my Japanese-American fiancée, would suffer the effects of the collective hate and fear of our nation.

I needed to let her know all was still right between us and we could survive the craziness that had overcome the world.

After a much longer silence, the voice of Bill Glasscock, our building supervisor, came over the speakers.

"Gentlemen, Commander Munson's orders are to expand production to the maximum extent possible. All leave has been cancelled. With the battleships out of action, our war in the Pacific, for the moment, will be largely dependent on submarines and carrier-based torpedo planes. Starting today, the work week will go from five days on, two days off to eight days on, two days off. Shifts will be extended from eight-to ten-hour days.

"There goes my wedding date," I said to Andy.

Glasscock continued. "Because of the vital nature of our work here at Keyport, physical security will be increased. Carry your photo ID badge with you at all times. We will be taking names of volunteers willing to be trained as a reserve force to defend the station should we come under attack. Sign-up sheets will be posted in the locker room. The station will be observing a mandatory blackout between twilight and dawn, starting today. Be on the lookout for suspicious persons inside and outside the station. Remember, information is a weapon for our enemy, so don't give him anything to use against us."

I passed through our locker room and joined the line already forming to volunteer for the station's auxiliary defense force. As I left the locker room with my lunch box in hand, I saw workmen installing footings outside the main door of the building.

"What's up, guy?"

"Blackout, pal. You don't want a Jap spy or bomber pilot to see light when you open the door at night, do yah? We're putting up another exterior door and a little walkway leading into the building. We'll have it done today, so don't worry."

Looking up over my left shoulder, I located the strange sounds that had caught my interest. Up on the roof, workmen were attaching heavy brown tarps. By the end of the shift—through the wall of windows that provided natural light for my delicate work—I saw the tarps descend. Blackout curtains—so we could work longer at making weapons to kill Japs, while the Japs supposedly looked for our tell-tale lights to sight their bombs or their deck guns. The curtains descending over our windows seemed to match the darkness covering the light in our once-sunny nation.

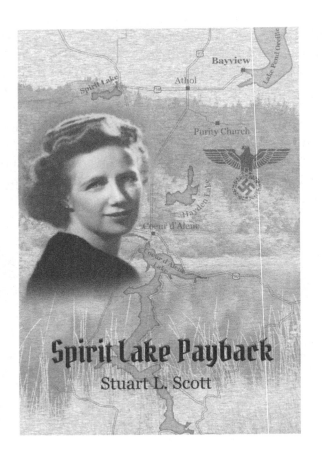

Available at Amazon in paperback and on Kindle
ISBN: 978-1-7322468-6-7

Sample from *Spirit Lake Payback*

Prologue: Spokane, Washington

June 6, 1995

The Spokane newspaper article ran under the banner, **Residents Rush to Plug Leaky Lake.**

"It was only last week that this reporter's boat was in the water, but now it's beached on weeds and mud, here next to my dock. State officials aren't sure why the lake is leaking, but they know it's leaking a lot of water into the Spokane aquifer. The state believes that holes are the main problem. The spokesman for the Idaho Department of Lands explained. 'It's tough to tell legitimate holes from the occasional moose footprint, or one dug by a toad when the lakebed was dry. The trick is to stir up some muck near a suspected hole. If it gets sucked down, the hole is declared a "leaker" and resealed. Unless you see it happen, it's hard to believe.'"

June 10, 1995

Today the follow-up newspaper headline was an eye catcher. **Spirit Lake Sink Hole Collapses to Reveal Skeletal Remains.**

"Idaho authorities interrupted the efforts of local homeowners to seal the continuing plague of sink holes when an undetermined number of human skeletons were discovered in the bottom muck of a collapsed sink hole. A 250 ft. area on the south shore of the lake has been cordoned off. State and tribal archeologists are preparing to excavate the site, hoping to determine the provenance of the apparent ancient burial ground."

June 30, 1995

Spirit Lake Sink Hole Linked to Mob Body Dump.

The Kootenai County Sheriff in his lakeside press conference revealed, "Those remains appear to be 40 to 60 years old and not a tribal burial ground as we first imagined. The archeological excavation has yielded up scraps of clothing and shoes that confirm the approximate age of the remains. The Coeur d'Alene tribal Archeologist called us in yesterday when he removed a skull from the pit and noticed fillings and gold teeth. Once the site is excavated, the identification of the remains will begin. Until that time, we have a bit of a mystery on our hands."

A combined local, state and federal multi-agency task force recovered nine bodies from their Spirit Lake dump site. Skeletal remains had become disarticulated into a pile of anonymous bones, awaiting re-assembly. When they were dumped was a mystery, but bullet holes in many of the skulls and cut marks on bones all pointed to violent ends for the nine unknowns.

ENTREPRENEURSHIP
101

START A
BUSINESS

A WINERY CASE STUDY

STUART L. SCOTT

Why should you read this book? Do you want to start your own business, sell a product, or provide a valuable service? **Do you have a new business,** especially a small business? Do you like the idea of **learning from the insights and mistakes of others**? If you answered **YES** to any of these questions, then this book is for you. I learned long ago that I didn't have to be nearly as smart or creative, if I could steal the good ideas of others. This is your chance to do the same!

Available at Amazon in paperback and on Kindle

ISBN:9781732246843

Made in the USA
Columbia, SC
07 August 2022

64795560R00117